B

Cover Design: Canva original – Sadie Goodloe

Scripture quotations are taken from the BIBLE...

Scripture quotations marked (NIV) New International Version, (NLT) New Living Translation, (KJV) King James Version and (NKJV) New King James Version are taken from the Holy Bible referenced on Bible Hub. Copyright © 2004 – 2024 Bible Hub.

Good Therapy. (2007-2023). Some Possible Definitions of Love Include. Love. Goodtherapy.org/blog/psychpedia/love.

Mayo Clinic. (1998-2024). Mental Illness. Mayo Clinic. Mayoclinic.org/diseases-conditions/mental-illness.

Center for Disease Control and Prevention, CDC. (2023, April). Mental Health. CDC. www.cdc.gov/mentalhealth/learn.

Code Ninjas. www.codeninjas.com. Accessed 1 March 2023.

Google Translator. www.translate.google.com. Accessed March 2023

Winans, CeCe. "Never Lost" Believe for It. 2021. YouTube.

Hatfield, Bobby. "Unchained Melody" Righteous Brothers. 1965. YouTube.

Hash, James C. Sr. (2018-2019) Bishop Hash. St. Peters Church & World Outreach Center. Sermon inspirations.

Goodloe, Sadie
Sirens / Sadie Goodloe
ISBN 979-8-9898408-1-6
1.Christian fiction

Dedicated to the memory of my big sister Calandra McLean and niece TaShonna Cameron.

Always in my heart!

There is always a scripture for every obstacle we encounter in our lives. My hope is that this work of fiction, which is sprinkled with the word of God, continues to remind us that we have always been at the forefront of God's thoughts, as evident in His word.

Dedication

Discipline

Obedience

Chapter 1

Sierra Kerner was a believer. She knew God could and would, but it depended on what she would believe when she would believe what all God was and is capable of. All that determines when she would stop worrying. Because whether Sierra believed or not, God will and can. She knew this but refused to let the situation go. She refused to operate in her faith. She refused to recognize *who's* she was.

Sierra was wasting time and energy on something that was out of her reach as far as controlling the outcome. For if God is the beginning and the end then He already controls the outcome. For He is love, power, and wisdom, and if He is all that then we should not be afraid of the situation before us. Because God Loves us enough to want the absolute best for us. His wisdom surpasses all understanding. He knows what is best for us better than we know or could want for ourselves. And not least He is Power. He controls all, He has the last say. His power covers us all.

Sierra had to release it so she could be in a position to operate in what she was meant to operate in. She was not available to be used at full capacity.

"Set yourself free."

"Open-up for your blessing."

"Let go of your issues and allow God to do his thing."

"The Holy Spirit will always warn because God is always in control."

These phrases were on post-it-notes stuck to Sierra's bathroom mirror. Like hashtags, easily searchable, they were daily reminders of God's faithfulness and fuel to feed her faith.

As she brushed her teeth, she thought about another phrase she'd recently heard that stood out to her. While listening to a podcast on positive faith by plastic surgeon Dr. Nneamaka Nwubah, the doctor talked about how she battled against negative self-talk while in medical school. She said, "Be so confident about God's plan that you don't even get upset anymore when things don't go your way!". As she wiped the toothpaste from her lips and put on a fresh coat of lip gloss, she thought, not only do I need a post-it for my bathroom mirror but also one for my desk. Dr. Nneamaka was preaching on that one!

Before walking out the door she stopped in the foyer and read one of her favorite scriptures from the open bible:

Deuteronomy 6:4 "Hear, O Israel: The Lord our God, the Lord is one! 5Love the Lord your God with all your heart and with all your soul and with all your strength. 6These commandments that I give you today are to be on your hearts. 7Impress them on your children. Talk about them when you sit at home and when you walk along the road, when you lie down and when you get up...." Moses' reminder to the new generation of Israelites...

Then she said aloud as she walked out the door, Thank you, God, for loving me in spite of me!

Chapter 2

Back at home things were hectic. The phone seemed to ring all the time. No, not from bill collectors always calling but from family and friends always calling wanting something. See Sierra and her husband were blessed. Money was not an issue. Not that they were rich or anything, but their cup did runneth over, and where possible, they contributed to different causes to help others: Make a Wish Foundation, Relay for Life, and Victory Junction just to name a few. They were little league team parent coaches, volunteered on missions, and tithed into their church. Whatever they could, they did. But Sierra had another problem that hindered her from being available to operate in the things God intended. That is, she was always too available to others. No, not strange. She was Doctor Sierra to many family members and close friends. Always listening to their problems and suggesting resolutions. Taking on issues at any time of the day, like she was God himself. She put up no restraints and eventually those that she loved and cared for soon began to take advantage of her thoughtful ear.

Putting herself first was never a thought, but it was definitely something she needed to consider. Her best friend Jo from work seemed to always have something going on where she needed or at least wanted Sierra to listen and advise her. Jo, a single parent of a fourteen-year-old son, was an extremely attractive blond in her late thirties. She was 5'6" with a petite frame but a very seductive wardrobe that showcased a set of double D's. Most guys in the ER could not keep their eyes off her. Believe it or not, if she would just cover those things up Sierra thought, we wouldn't be having these conversations every Monday morning. "Sierra, I'm telling you he never looked me in my face. I just couldn't believe he had the nerve to stare at my girls all night like that." Sierra turned to pour some coffee and rolled her eyes, thinking, girl, yeah right! As she turned back around Jo continued, "Ed seemed like such a nice guy when we spoke on the phone after running into each other in the ER vending area at building C. We were just instantly drawn to each other. He looked me dead in the eye and slipped his number into my hand whispering... call me. He didn't even peep at my girls. Sierra, why does this always happen to me?" Jo whined. "Am I going to be single forever? I have a pre-teen with an absent father. I can't make his dad take time out for him and I just can't seem to make a connection with a decent man for my sons' sake... or for myself. Oh Sierra, what should I do?"

"Jo, I've told you before that when you stop looking for Mr. Right, Mr. Right will find you. You can only do what you're capable of doing. Just continue to love and support your son in all he does. Even if you find a man who doesn't think your girls as you put it, are one of the seven wonders of the world, who's to say that guy will be ready to become an instant dad to a pre-teen? First and foremost is your family, which consists of you and your son. Stop seeking the perfect man and the perfect man for your readymade family will find you." Sierra had done it again. She let her have it without totally letting go because the Christ in her wanted to say, seek ye first the Kingdom of God and all his righteousness and all these things (desired/needed) shall be added unto you. But of course, she suppressed that yearning within to do His will to do her own will. Like she did so many times... she ignored direction... inner direction.

She knew she was wasting her time because she and Jo had had this same conversation many times before. Jo was feeling desperate for a man to complete her family and it didn't seem as though she would stop anytime soon until she got what she sought.

Jo was just one of the people who frequently called Sierra for advice. And like Sierra did for Joe, she also took the time to listen to the other calls. From her mom, Rose, to sister Bre, cousin Rita, and Aunt Bella. From sister Green at church always complaining about something the ushers didn't do, to coworkers like Jo, who happened to be a friend at work to coworkers who worked in that wing of the ER. Sounds like a lot of problems, doesn't it? It was. One would wonder when a lady like Sierra had the time to listen to all those problems and still be an effective wife, mother, servant, volunteer, and MRO

Buyer for one of the largest hospitals in northwest Arizona.
Thinking aloud, "Let me get back to work, Jo; chat later,
Chicka!"

Chapter 3

Sierra's office was just one hall away from the canteen. So, she didn't have far to go. "I only meant to slide down to the canteen, get some coffee and head back. Needed my morning pickup... Got sidetracked once again. I need to have better control. Sierra was a very practical person and her wardrobe reflected that. Her soft-soled black penny loafers lightly patted the floor of the ER wing as she headed down the halls back to her office. Her waist-high black slacks fit her 5'10" medium frame to a T. And her wrist length button up white dockers dress shirt with black vest finished off her polished look. The only accessories that adorned her were a simple pair of platinum diamond earrings and her platinum crumb sized diamond wedding ring.

Finally arriving back at her desk, she immediately got to work.

"Judy...Judy! Page Sierra for me and ask that she come down to meet with me for a brief second to discuss this Coastal Project, Thank you!" Tom Black had been with West Arizona Hospital - WAH for over twenty years. He was a well-respected senior buyer who was promoted to Materials Manager eight years ago. He was small in frame but large in presence. His voice was very deceptive compared to his appearance. It boomed and reverberated around the office and out the door to Judy's desk daily. Always ringing out some request, and always ending with a Thank You! Tom was a man of great character and believed in treating others like he wanted to be treated, which made working for him an interesting experience every day.

Upon hearing his request Judy called Sierra and asked if she would come to Toms office, when she had a moment, Tom wanted to talk to her about the Coastal Project. Sierra made no hesitation; she had a moment; "I'll be down in 5 Judy". As she put down the phone Sierra turned to the shelf behind her that held her Coastal Project notebook. She took a quick moment to review her notes. Let me see where I am now. I'm sure Tom wants to know where the projects at. Give him the facts, she thought. As she flipped through the pages, reviewing her notes from the last five months of work, she took long exaggerated deep breaths to relax before the meeting. It was essential to be relaxed in Tom's presence. He is so hyper that he constantly moves even when sitting, and his anxious movement can sometimes make the listener nervous or uneasy. Knowing this, Sierra realized there was no reason to be nervous, she only needed to be prepared. Whispering a quick prayer, Father, I want to thank you for this day, for my health and strength, for the ability of my limbs, for the abundance of peace, a sound mind, and peace granted to me today. Thank you for this job and for the opportunity to be a light and a representation of you in the workplace. I ask that you go before me and give me peace during this meeting and that you be my mouthpiece and speak for me as I converse with my boss Tom. In Jesus name... Amen. As she took one last deep breath, she pushed away from her desk, closed the notebook, and stood... here we go, she said as she headed towards Tom's office.

The Coastal Project had become her baby. Sierra was proud of the fact that Tom had given her responsibility as project lead. The project's scope was to relocate or help set up three WAH major international vendors along the western coast of the US. Target areas are Seattle, WA, Portland, OR, and San Francisco, CA. Surnegel, who is out of Japan, has already agreed to move into the Seattle region. Surnegel is WAH's major provider of syringes, needles, and numbing gels. Yars out of Taiwan is under contract to begin building a new facility in Portland. They produce X-ray films. Newman Cast has yet to commit to relocating to the States. The goal is to get them into the San Francisco area. Newman produces all WAH's cast and bandage materials. "Hi, Judy", Sierra whispered as she passed Judy's desk and headed into Tom's office. Judy turned toward Sierra, smiled, and nodded, "hi Sierra". Tom looked up from his computer as she entered his office. "Come on in" he said as he minimized all work on his computer leaving just a picture of his two boys smiling back at him on the screen. "How are things going Sierra?" "All is well", she responded in her best professional tone. "Great. I was just wondering how the

Coastal Project was coming along"? "Things are coming along", she started". "Surnegel is currently looking for a facility somewhere in the Seattle region. In my last meeting with Mel, He' San, he stated that they have narrowed their search down to two facilities and should have a pick by mid-October". Looking at the date on her Apple watch, "which is in about a week." "Mr. Yomen Littlea of Yars has already purchased land in the San Francisco countryside and is now under contract with builders to begin construction." "Mr. Littlea communicated in our bi-weekly meeting that they should break ground by November first". Tom shook his head up and down, well pleased that things were moving ahead of schedule. He was also jumping his legs up and down under his desk, but of course, Sierra ignored his nervous habit and continued. "We are still waiting on Mrs. Liz Bonga from Newman Cast to finish their review of the business agreement and commit to relocating one of their business units to the states. During our bi-weekly meeting, I pressed Newman Cast to be prepared to give us a decision: yea or nea by October first". Tom raised an eyebrow looking puzzled, then calmly said, "Sierra, you mean Liz has not even agreed to move a unit to the states? Liz is forever dragging her feet to make a decision. We are five months into this project, and they are still reviewing the business plan. Okay, we will give them until the first of October. If they can't tell us anything one way or another," he said while clicking his blue gel pen in and out, "then I am going to have to give them a call." "I understand," Sierra said aloud while thinking please stop it with the pen. Tom then laid the pen down and put his hands together and laid them atop the desk, then said, "Well done so far, now let's keep this ball rolling until the project is complete". "I'll do my best." Tom turned back to his computer. Sierra knew that was her queue to leave. Securing her notebook under her arm she got up and left feeling like strawberries and lemonade on a warm summer night.

On her way back to her desk, she said a small prayer, thanking God for giving her the nudging to prepare before that meeting. I can do all things through you God... Amen, she said as she sat back down at her desk to begin her day.

Chapter 4

"Rice again." "Yes, rice again. It's good chicken-flavored rice, your favorite." She chuckled to herself as she prepared the dinner plates for supper. What a little investigator I have on my hand. Max, her ten-year-old son, was always questioning everything from why the man's sign read 'Why lie I need a beer' to if we are having rice again if so, what flavor tonight. Max was a great son. Handsome like his father. A thin medium frame, with a smooth chocolate complexion. He had bright, round marble-sized eyes that held the color of the deep, murky gray ocean. Eyes that held a very curious expression behind schoolboy wireframe glasses. He couldn't help but be tall for ten since his mom and dad were both considered tall at 5'10" and 6'4". Even though Sierra gave birth to this curious kid he still amazed her often. So inquisitive about life and so present in every moment. "I bet you can't guess what I bought for dessert tonight?" Sierra said to Max as she sat down beside him at the dinner table after putting his plate and hers on the table. Max looked at his plate before answering. "Broccoli and cheese, baked chicken with smothered gravy, chicken flavored rice... mmmmm," Max said with a pleased look on his face. "I love baked chicken smothered in gravy!"

Sierra smiled back at him while waiting for him to answer her question. "Let us bless this food. Most holy and all mighty God, Sierra started aloud, we ask that you bless this food for the nourishment of our bodies. We ask that it strengthens our physical bodies and not harm it, so that we might go about our father's business. In Jesus name, we pray, Amen." "Amen," Max echoed. "So," Sierra said, "guess what's for dessert tonight." "Mum?" Max said between bites of his chicken, "Butter pecan ice cream" he said. No, that's your other favorite thing she thought to herself. "I bought strawberries from the farmers market on the way home today." He smiled; "I should have known it was fruit. It is that time of the year. The end of spring means the start of strawberry season," Max mouthed as he smacked on his rice. "While you were finishing your homework, I cut up strawberries, sprinkled them with sugar, and put them in the fridge to chill. They should be just right by the time we finish our meal." Which would be in no time for Max considering he was finishing off the pile of broccoli and cheese, the last thing on his plate. "Mom, that was great. I was hungry too. The lunch at school wasn't good today so I didn't eat much."

He got up, put his plate in the sink, then sat back down with Sierra while she finished her food. Half a minute of silence passed before he asked if his dad would make it back tonight from his business trip to Mexico. "No baby, I spoke with your father today at the office. He said the job he and his team contracted for was running over schedule. Instead of pulling out and heading home today, they wouldn't complete the job until Friday. So not many more days," she said as she reached across and tapped him on his nose with her index finger as she often did. Just two more days and he will be home. "I know you miss him when he goes away on those business trips but that's his job. He worked hard starting his company, Maxwell Construction LLC 9 years ago to get it to where it is today. You were his driving force little man. He wanted to make sure he could provide for us and that he does. Now go get the strawberries out the fridge; I'm ready for some dessert," she smiled, then wiped her mouth with a paper napkin from the roll in the center of the table.

Sierra didn't have to tell Max twice. Again, she smiled at him while clearing off the table and grabbing some paper plates. By the time she returned to the table, Max was there with the bowl of berries and whipped cream of course. They ate berries and talked about their day until it was time for Max's bath. Not many more weeks, she reminded him, before school would be out for the summer. Max couldn't wait!

Chapter 5

Maxwell Jerohim Kerner, owner of Maxwell Construction LLC, was a man of integrity, faith, and a deep love for God. At 6'4", medium muscular build with broad square shoulders and a very distinctive mellow baritone voice, it was hard for him to blend into any crowd. Good thing he didn't need to blend in. He was a man of character that everyone liked and respected. Loved by his family, including his five brothers, and respected by his diverse fifteen-man crew.

MJ, as most called him, always took the time to get to know everyone he encountered at some level. He believed the words his grandfather, who was also a gentle giant, always spoke;" be kind to everyone – you never know when you may be entertaining angles. Which works hand in hand with loving thy neighbor which pleases God". Last thing MJ wanted to do was dishonor God or miss an opportunity to be a host in God's honor.

MJ missed his family and was sooo ready to go home and kiss his wife and hug his son. He was grateful to God for giving him a family to love and care for. 'In due time," he whispered to himself. First thing first... finish this project. His crew was completing two weeks of stuccoing the front of seven homes in a new development in New Mexico. Being picked for the project was a huge step for Maxwell Construction, their second big job outside Arizona. They were well known throughout Arizona for completing jobs of high quality yet cost-efficient. If you could define it under the construction title, then Maxwell Construction could do it. Homes, industrial buildings, outside structures, light fixtures they did it all. MJ believed starting somewhere was better than doing nothing at all. So, if it was a light fixture in your home or a beam in a warehouse, MJ bid on the job. It got his foot in the door and helped him build an incredibly good network of references. Thank God for references, they helped him secure the loan he needed to buy the capital equipment needed to expand Maxwell Construction. Now that he can afford to employ more than Ricco Ortega, his company is equipped to conquer bigger jobs in competitive time frames, which is a particularly important factor when it comes to winning major jobs. This job in New Mexico was a big win for them. He and Ortega had been friends for years, they both had a passion for creating, building and improving.

Ortega is known for his craftiness in electrical. He's quick, neat, and always up on code. They met on a job site many years ago. At the time MJ was finishing up the plumbing for Handyman's Recruits at the new Lowes back home in Opng, Arizona. He was certified in all things construction but working through the staffing service. None of the jobs ever seemed to last longer than a year through Handyman's. MJ was fed up with the lack of additional benefits, things like health insurance, life insurance, or even a retirement plan. He knew he had responsibilities as a husband and dad, so he took work even for a staffing service. Unbeknownst to MJ, Ortega felt the same way. He hated having to constantly work for Handyman's Recruits, but it was putting bread on the table. He, too, had a family. He loved dearly his wife Maria and simply adored his four girls. Another apparent reason why the job he worked wasn't important as long as he worked. Feeding those five mouths was his ultimate goal after pleasing God. For God was his Alpha and Omega his beginning and his end. He depended totally on God for his everything. He knew without God he wouldn't be able to provide for his family. God had been good to him. As he grew in the Lord Ortega knew God was pulling and stretching him, preparing him for something great. He just needed to step back and focus on God so He could show him exactly what that something was. So, while he waited on God, he renewed his mind on God's word. This was exactly what he was doing the day he met MJ.

Ortega was enjoying his fried bologna sandwich his wife made for lunch while reclining against a stack of sheetrock at the Lowes job site Handyman's had sent him to. He was reading the book of Jeremiah, meditating on one of his favorites versus. Chapter 32 verse 27: (KJV) "Behold, I am the Lord the God of all Flesh. Is there anything too hard for Me?" His spirit answered, No Lord …. Nothing is too hard for you. And he really believed that word with all his heart. He also knew God was dealing/ministering to his most inner spirit. Ortega had plans or thoughts of starting his own construction business; however, as much as he loved and trusted God he battled against himself. Fear, which he knew was not of God kept him from moving his feet. So, on top of meditating on God's word, Ortega also stayed in prayer for himself… asking God for the boldness to move forward with his plan and, at the same time, forgiveness for not trusting God wholeheartedly. Things God had for him were yet to be seen. If he would only move on what he knew God could do, things in his life would be different.

God knows the heart. What God saw was the heart of a man who wanted more so he could do more for his family. Not to fluff himself up but to provide better for his four girls and wife. Ortega really wanted to work for himself, be his own boss, bid his own jobs, and complete them on a more efficient time scale with better designs. He had a lot of ideas on this, and at some point, he knew that he needed to move on his thoughts and be obedient in the small things like trusting God. So in between bits of his lunch, his head was bowed, his back was against the wall of the floor he was working on, his bible in his lap… he spoke with God. Ortega thanked God for providing this job, waking him up, and giving him a loving wife and mentally healthy little girls. He thanked him for transportation and favor with men... for waking him up that very day and for keeping him safe up to that very moment on his job. During his worship within his thirty-minute lunch break, he shabached God with his praise of enduring words. God is awesome; He is excellent, omnipotent, his provider, his protector, and the man with the final say in all things. As he said "Amen" and lifted his head he noticed a tall black guy coming his way. As he stood to greet him, MJ extended his hand to introduce himself.

"Ortega". MJ said in a questioning tone. "Yes, I'm Ricco Ortega," he said with a warm smile. For his spirit was at peace from his brief worship and his physical countenance reflected it. MJ immediately saw his helmet of salvation in the spirit. "Taking some time to sharpen your sword, eh? I can already see you're my kind of guy; a man of God." MJ went on to introduce himself to Ortega, including how he had come to hear of him. Ortega listened as MJ spoke... showing the fruits of the spirit - patients. But wondering where all of this was coming from. "Yes, I heard from many that you are one of the best-known 'unknown' electricians around. You see, I'm preparing to go into business for myself, and I am looking for a good electrician who may want to come along for the ride or possibly partner". Now he had Ortega's attention though he didn't know it. "Oh yeah? Man, we should definitely get together after work or tomorrow during lunch so you can give me the full details. I have a big family, so I am always looking to improve our status". MJ liked what he heard. While shaking Ortega's hand and smiling they agreed to get together tomorrow after work to discuss further. As they say... the rest is history. Less than three months later, they were in agreement on the business plan for Maxwell Construction LLC. Ortega would be the electrical manager. However, the business would be in MJ's name since Ortega had no assets. Their business flourished in Arizona, and both families prospered.

Chapter 6

"The blessing of the Lord makes one rich, and He adds no sorrow with it," Sierra read the cafeteria ladies' button while waiting in line to check out.

She seemed to be in a daze today. "Wow," she thought while standing there, "that is so true." As she inched toward the register, she saw the scripture referenced... Proverbs 10:22 (KJV) in ridiculously small print at the bottom of the big button. She smiled and paid for her salad and can of Coke Zero then sat down at her favorite table in the corner. Proverbs 10:22: she kept repeating the verse; she'd only brought money to the café for lunch leaving her purse locked in her desk. I must tag that verse in my bible so I can meditate on it when needed. This time, she repeated it out loud, "Proverbs 10:22" and took a bite of her food and looked up. "Mind if I sit here with you pretty lady"? "Sure, Dr. Loveatounge". Joe had to take her son to get a sports physical, so I was kicking it solo today". "I noticed which is why I took the opportunity to come right on over. It's normally very hard to get this close to you". Sierra caught herself holding her breath at Dr. Loveatounge's statement. Then she continued to breathe rhythmically as he finished with, "Joe normally have you at lunchtime, your staff during the day, Tom mid-day, closed door in the evening and then poof – you're gone." Sierra sat back in her chair, very stunned, and stared at this doctor like he had lost his mind. Dr.

Loveatounge happened to catch her expression after looking up from biting into his burger. Bingo... got her attention, he thought! Smiling and chewing, he looked at Sierra, head cocked to the side, "Yes, I keep up with you, Ms. Kerner". I see, she thought! "Mr. Lo." "No, call me Greg". "Greg, what can I help you with"?

Sierra felt she said it in her most professional tone but the way Dr. Loveatounge was looking at her, all bright eyes, his expression was somewhere between a smile and surprise, she wasn't really sure. "I like that Sierra; can I call you Sierra? You carry yourself well, so well-spoken, quick on your feet, and ever so pleasant; even when you're uncomfortable. Forgive my frankness but I have been wanting to sit with you and get to know you better for some time. The lady from accounting seems to always have your ear at lunch. Joe, is it? Well, I'm glad Joe had other plans today". Sierra decided to take it from here. "So, Greg what's going on in the Pediatric unit today? I haven't seen you in a while around here. Guess that's why I was a little taken aback by you reciting my schedule. When do you have time to keep up with anyone or anything if it's not going down in Pediatrics? Your unit stays very busy up there". "You know how men do; we keep tabs on what we want. Either way, I am just messing with you, Sierra. I just wanted to sit with someone at lunch today. Opportunity knocked so I stepped on in. I just know of you; thought I'd take the time to actually get to know you". Ohhhh...kay, wow, doc you really threw me for a loop there. He's surfing for something I know it, she thought. "Dr. Lov... I mean Greg. You work all the time. Do you have anyone to spend your free time with, like family"? "Yes, I have been married for five years now. Married my college sweetheart". "Any kids"? "No kids. At one time we planned to have a house overflowing with a few girls for me and little boys for her, but that was then". Sierra sensed that Greg was getting sadder and sadder as he spoke. She wanted to inquire more but... this was her lunch haven, and she was in a decent mood and wanted to keep it that way, so she interjected. "Well, I have one kid, Max. He's ten, but I think that maybe it. Max is a great kid. He keeps me and my husband busy with his traveling band outings and he's a hilarious little fella". Smiling, Greg questioned more about Max's band extracurricular activities. "What instrument does he play"? "Trumpet, he's pretty awesome at it", Sierra said while smiling back at Greg. "Traveling band at ten, that's different", Greg continued smiling. Sierra thought what a nice smile, those are some pearly whites... he is Dr. Loveatounge.

Sierra went on to explain that at the local rec center near her house, they started the band at the beginning of the year. Many kids had turned up after the announcement via flyer was posted. Enough kids for a twenty-five-piece band. "They range in age from ten to fourteen, mostly middle schoolers, and practice once a week. Max is one of the youngest. Per Dr. Size, their band director, he thought they were good enough to go out-and-about to different community events. So that's what they do, volunteering their sound".

"That's wonderful, maybe we can get the band up to the Pediatric unit one day. I am sure the kids in the unit would love that. Dr. Greg said between gulps of milk". "I'm sure Dr. Size would be open to the invitation", Sierra said crossing her arms. "Well, Sierra, thanks for the company... allowing me to sit with you that is. I really enjoyed the convo. Normally I come get something to eat and head back to my office, eating alone in solace. I enjoyed the change in routine". "Anytime, Dr. Greg", smiled Sierra. "It's normally Joe and I but you're welcome to join us anytime for lunch. You seem to have my schedule and local locked on your internal GPS. So, you know where to find us". Greg laughed, almost looking a little ashamed that he had revealed all he did earlier. "Yes, Sierra ha ha ha. I know where you be; as the kids would say, thanks for the open invite". He said all this as he got up, pushed the chair back under the table, turned, and left. Sierra shook her head and silently thought, "just like that the wind blew in and right back out. Just a tad bit strange but intriguing at the same time. Keep me informed Holy Ghost. I feel there's more to come from that encounter".

And on that thought Sierra got up, piled her trash on her tray, wiped the table with her napkins (which was an OCD habit she hated exhibiting) and exited the café dumping her trash on the way out. She glimpsed at the clock hanging above the nice cafeteria ladies' head on the way out; 1:01 pm.

She had a meeting with WAH's sourcing team at 1:15 pm and needed to return to her office. "Have a blessed day mam", the lady with the button said. "You too," said Sierra with a smile as she took in God's message once more. Mouthing the scripture as she read it silently, the blessing of the Lord makes one rich, and He adds no sorrow with it! "Amen", she said, "amen!"

Chapter 7

"Hola amigos! Es la habitacion completa"? Ortega was addressing the workers on his floor. All of which happened to be of Hispanic descent. "Si jefe, esta completamente completo", the oldest of the gentleman replied. "Great, you guys do great work and finish ahead of schedule. Now that's a great way to end this week and this project. I'll ensure you guys are taken care of. Your work speaks for itself". "Gracies," they all said as they left the room.

Ortega loved working with anyone whose number one focus was to get the job done. He walked through the room doing a final check. The inspector would be through early in the AM. He and MJ were ready to go back home to their families.

Two weeks in New Mexico was one week too long. If they didn't pass inspection on tomorrow it wouldn't be until Monday until the inspector could get back out. That would be expensive. It would mean another weekend in NM for him, MJ, and their crew. So, he inspected the circuits, outlets, switches, and the cleanliness of it all. He then checked his code book once more to ensure all spacing was correct. This many inches from the floor... hum, that many from the doorway. As he went around once more checking the measurements with his measuring tape, he meditated on scripture, Hebrew 10:38... "now the just shall live by faith, but if any man draws back, my soul shall have no pleasure in him." By the time he had checked the third outlet in the master bedroom, he had repeated this scripture fifteen times.

Ortega was really zoning in on the word 'just.' Was he just, did that include him? He knew he was taking hold of the promises of God for him and his family but was he where he needed to be in Christ? That weighed on him heavily. He tried to live holy. Assuming 'just' was holy. Pulling out his phone, he clicked on the web browser, going to dictionary.com, where he typed in the word 'just'. The first definition read, 'guided by truth, reason, justice, and fairness,' the next one read 'based on right, rightful, lawful.' "Lawful, do I govern myself by God's law? I do in every possible way, I do", he told himself. "I try my best", he said aloud. Frowning now as he clicked off the browser and put the phone back in his pocket..., "I try God"! Still frowning, "I really do, even though Lord...". Turning to take one last glance around the room... "even though I struggle over control with You of this temple" pointing at himself "this body". "I trust You for everything", he said aloud to God. "My faith is strong".

This room is done he thought and ready for inspection. I'll just run to the porta-john and take a quick break he thought. As he trampled down the stairs a still sweet voice whispered; "do you not know that your body is a temple of the Holy Spirit ..." (1 Cor. 6:19). Continuing to frown, Ortega didn't change strides or his pace. Now on the main floor he heard it repeated... "Do you not know ... of the Holy Spirit." Exiting the front door, he stopped outside the entrance.

Telling himself, "I'm fine, I don't need a break. It's just 11 am". Adding, "I'm a just man trying to exercise my faith." He patted the pocket on the inside of his coat. "Yeah, no break needed right now," he said looking obsessed and upset. Still standing at the entrance, he looked down at his boots (the feet belonging to God) and patted his pocket again. "Why do I struggle so with my flesh God"? He said to himself. As he glanced to his left, he spotted the porta-john. In an instant, his destination was once again lodged on his radar, and before he knew it, he was in the john, locked the door, and pulled out his weapon of choice. His struggle, the thing that seemed to have a grip so strong on his flesh not even the Jaws of Life seemed to be able to remove it. Out came the pipe, out came the powdery substance and lighter.

In that filthy porta-john, at 11 in the morning, Ortega slowly slid to the floor from the toilet. Mumbling... "God I try to live by faith... I want to be just... my family...Oh God, my family".

For the next twenty minutes, Ortega occupied the john on his break in a drug-induced comatose state.

Chapter 8

Bishop Give took the podium to pray. MJ has his head bowed, but his eyes were open, enjoying the sight of his growing son Max, standing to his left. "Getting really tall," he said to himself. Last time Max wore those pants to church, they were gathered on top of his shoes. Now they are barely touching his shoes, MJ thought chuckling. And to his right stood his wife Sierra. So put together he thought – always so neat. He loved that about his wife. Squeezing her hand while Bishop Give ended the prayer – they looked up in unison, warmly smiled at each other, and sat down.

So glad to have made it home from New Mexico mid-day Saturday; he was the first one up this morning, ready to go and give God his praise. Lifting his hand in the sanctuary, during worship, MJ thanked God for his family, friends, and work crew, for his going down and coming back from New Mexico safely. Thanked the Father for being the Father and for His Son Jesus. And now that Bishop Give, the senior pastor at New World Same God Life Church, was beginning to minister, he was looking forward to receiving this word. As MJ finally stopped smiling at his family and tuned into what Bishop Give was ministering about, he began to take notes ... "my responsibility requires a spirit of faithfulness, never giving up, and depending on God- God always clarifies our responsibilities so we can respond in obedience." MJ circled that one. "Good word Bishop'" he shouted. "Amen", Sierra confirmed. MJ continued to write as Bishop Give continued, "God will never leave or forsake you, and he promises to shoulder the responsibility with you". "God", Bishop Give boomed as he walked across the podium, "always prepares us for our assignments. Let me say that again", Bishop said pointing to his PowerPoint projected on the screen pitched high above his head directly behind the choir stand. "God ALWAYS," he said with emphasis, "prepares us for our assignment". "What an awesome God we serve church"! "All right let me move on... my time is winding up". "Three keys to being a responsible person.

1 – Confidence in Gods calling and ability

2 – Courage to obey regardless of the cost

3 - Commitment to God"

"Study on that church, and we will pick up here next Sunday."

As Bishop made the alter call MJ wrapped up his notes. He intended to meditate on those three principles. Putting everything back in his bible tote, he zipped everything in. "Church, you are dismissed," Bishop Give announced.

Slowly standing and stretching Max announced he was ready to eat. MJ smiled and playfully gave Max a headlock hug as they exited the sanctuary. MJ was all smiles. He simply adored his family. He patiently waited as Sierra greeted Mother Green in the halls outside the sanctuary and in the same breath then turn to let Mother Smith know how lovely her silver church hat looked this late spring morning. He loved the respectful way she always honored the seniors in their church. His mother may not have done much at home for him and his brothers, but she always stressed for them to respect their elders if they wanted to live a good long life. And MJ thought as he smiled a little wider, showing off those pearly whites, giving Mother Smith an acknowledged hello with a nod of his head, it's just plain respectable and polite.

"Max, where should we stop to eat?" MJ asked as he pulled from the parking space and exited the church lot. "How about Reggie's Soul Food Plaza"? Frowning but still smiling MJ looked at Sierra. "How does he know about the Soul Food Plaza"? She shrugged her shoulders, "I have no idea". "Our community band played in the square across from the plaza during the city's rededication ceremony they had early this year." Oh yeah– that's right, Sierra thought, we were across the street from it.

"Dad I've been wanting to go in since I saw it. I've never eaten at a soul food restaurant before". "Okay," MJ said while looking in the review mirror, "Reggie's Soul Food Plaza it is"! Sierra turned up the radio to better hear the tune of her favorite gospel group, Mary-Mary, belting out Go Get Your Blessing.

MJ exited onto Interstate 40 to head downtown. By the time the Marys had completed the song MJ was one stop light away from the restaurant. "Wow, it's been a while since I've been downtown. The city has made a lot of cosmetic improvements! The area looks inviting, and it looks like others agree with me. All this traffic", MJ said as he patiently waited for their light to change. Sitting at the light and looking around, he suddenly thought he saw Ortega talking to a group of men standing in front of one of the abandoned buildings under construction. The light had turned green; however, MJ was not conscious of it. He was too busy straining to see if he was seeing what he thought he saw. "MJ, you have the light", Sierra said watching him watch Ortega! However, she didn't quite know what he was staring at. "Thanks, honey, little distracted there"? MJ pulled through the light into Reggie's Soul Food Plaza parking deck. He'd lost sight of the abandoned building, from where they were parked, but he was fairly sure that was Orgeta talking to those guys. "Alright, guys, let's go eat," MJ smiled at his family as they exited the car. The smell of ribs, buttered rice, gravy and fried cornbread was lingering in the air. They did just that, ate, enjoying a family lunch together at Reggie's on Sunday. Good food, conversation, atmosphere, and for MJ, thoughts of Ortega. Even though he was enjoying his family he couldn't get that scene out of his head. He knows what he thought he saw but he really wanted to know what Ortega was doing. He didn't want to speculate but he would surely find out.

Chapter 9

Sure looked like MJ downtown around lunchtime today. Hope it was not him. Scratching his head, Ortega assured himself that his eyes only thought he saw who he saw. Unwrapping his package, dropping in his tube he was on to the task at hand. This bit. He struck his lighter, took two puffs, and faded into his car seat... where he would be until the sun came up.

Maria found herself praying as she washed the dishes left from the evening's meal. She thoroughly enjoyed cooking for her big family. She and Ortega started their family young in New Mexico.

Born Maria Ruez, she was also from a big family. She was the seventh of seven siblings; even though she was the youngest, she always prepared meals along with her mother for the rest of the family. Her love of cooking evolved early, and she honed her skills as she continued to prepare meals for those she loved.

At Gadsden High School in New Mexico, Maria met Ricco Ortega her sophomore year. Ricco was a Junior. All elective classes were in one building on their high school campus. Maria was taking Home Economics, hoping to learn new nontraditional Hispanic recipes. Ricco was taking an advanced-level Electrical Shop class. He had always been intrigued with the power of electricity from an early age so jumped at the chance to sign up for Gadsden HS advanced shop classes, where the focus was on building electric cars. The day he ran into Maria he was hurrying to class, anxious because it was the first day his class was finally beginning to put theory into practice. The class had studied how electric cars were built and reviewed examples of successful electric builds but hadn't actually built an electric car.

Running to the elective building he stopped short of knocking Maria over when she was leaving the building, and he entered the building. "Hey, watch it hombre salvaje"! Maria frowned at him as she caught her balance. "Sorry," Ricco said as he stopped and held the door for her to exit. In that instant he mentally took her in, wondering why he hadn't seen her around before this year. Maybe she was new, he thought. She had an athletic build, about 5'8", jet black shoulder length hair, styled in a bob with a middle part that divided it symmetrically. Soft brown eyes that reflected a kindness that didn't match her current tone. All that was enough to spark an interest in Ricco. For now, he had to get to class and change into his shop uniform so he could get to work on his electric car. As she exited and he entered, he said "Bonita" in a sing-song manner out loud thinking she didn't hear him. She did hear him, and the rest is history.

They'd been together twenty years in February. Their oldest daughter was twelve and their youngest was four. She loved her family as much as she loved God. Maybe this was the reason she continued to give Ortega a pass, hoping not to rock the boat even though she felt something was not right. Chatting with the girls mid-week from New Mexico, she knew they were wrapping up the job and would be headed home, at the earliest, on Saturday. After all these years, the last thing she wanted to think was that he was cheating on their family with another woman. Yet again it was a Sunday evening dinner without him. She never questioned him when he finally did come home, and he never offered an explanation.

As she wiped down the countertops and stove, she thought about his relationship with their girls. They absolutely love their dad. Completely wrapped around their little fingers, they could talk their dad into almost anything. He constantly read to them from their favorite books and scriptures from his. He'd become an expert at their favorite card game, Dutch Blitz, and would prepare their favorite snack, toasted peanut butter and jelly sandwiches, on request. And for years, every Sunday morning before church, he would twist a single ponytail and add a bow. All the girls would giggle as he did this thinking it was funny seeing their dad fumble with the bows with his huge hands. For the last month, since Ortega returned from the first assignment in New Mexico, their Sunday morning routine did not start back. He'd not been at home any Sunday morning since he'd returned. Morning or evening. Lately, she didn't see him until around 7 pm Sunday nights which was around the time the girls were getting their baths preparing for school and daycare the next day.

Experiencing four different births, Maria was very aware of birthing pains. The uncomfortable feeling of something new, uniquely its own, breaking through the norm shifting your paradigm. Sometimes, the pain is easy, but the pressure of it is sometimes laborious. What life was is no longer: where there was one now there is another. Something was shifting in her, God preparing her, but she wasn't sure for what.

Selflessly she had catered to her husband's desire to do things his way. She'd said nothing to him when he entered the house at 7 pm on Sunday nights, only glancing his way waiting for him to explain himself. The explanation never came. The girls were so excited to see him, and he seemably them that she let it go. The sirens were blaring, 'Maria, something is not right'. Instead of addressing the issue she pivoted away from it, choosing to sprinkle the atmosphere with positive vibes and a smile that said I love my family on the outside while her heart was filling with anxiety on the inside. His checks were directly deposited, so household needs were taken care of but the void of not having her husband home was growing. Glancing up at the clock from deep in her thoughts she saw the clock chimed 9 pm. The girls were sound asleep, the house was quiet and there was no Ortega.

Chapter 10

There is a difference between loyalty and love. Loyalty is when you're committed to the relationship, to this joint thing we started some time ago, and now, years later, here we are. Loyalty can sometimes turn into tolerance. You begin to tolerate the person because the quantity of good characteristics outweighs the bad and yet that thing that would make tolerance evolve into love seems to be stacked on the terrible side of the scale. Then you start to notice that you're just being tolerated, not loved. Not always mistreated but dismissed when it counts. You start to realize it does not matter how many things you adjust, give selflessly, or deny yourself for this other person; it will never be enough. Because the essence of who you are is stacked on the bad side of the scale when they look at it.

Maria was starting to feel like she was being tolerated. It wasn't about being alone during the last two weeks when he was in New Mexico. She'd felt the absence of love for some time now.

Their encounters were robotic, routine, day in and day out. Going through the motions of life providing and caring for their family they lost their intimacy. They did what was expected not what was desired. A peck on the lips here and a kiss on the forehead occasionally but rarely an encounter filled with desire. Their love was more in the friend zone, but she desired more affectionate eros love.

Even though Ortega often said how much he loved his family, she also knew he was loyal to family. He is from a generation of men who were all very loyal to the family unit. She still couldn't shake the feeling that something was off!

It was late, she needed to go to sleep. Tomorrow was the start of another busy week. Looking to tire her mind, she pulled her laptop from the nightstand and googled the phrase, 'What is the meaning of love.' Seeing various articles, she was quickly drawn to a blog by Good Therapy (goodtherapy.org/blog/psychpedia/love). Chuckling to herself she thought, this is precisely what I need, some therapy. Skimming the article, she came to a section titled, "Some Possible Definitions of Love Include:

- A willingness to prioritize another's well-being or happiness above your own
- Extreme feelings of attachment, affection, and need
- Dramatic, sudden feelings of attraction and respect.
- A fleeting emotion of care, affection, and like
- A choice to commit to helping, respecting, and caring for another, such as in marriage or when having a child
- Some combination of the above emotions"

Some she thought sounded very much like loyalty. Feeling confused, she wondered if she was just not being loved the way Ortega was capable of loving. Or did he not love her and was only loyal to their family....so remained?

The author of the blog ended by declaring love is complex. Simply stated, he said that "it is a mix of emotions, behaviors, and beliefs associated with strong feelings of affection, protectiveness, warmth, and respect for another person." And Maria agreed; love is surely complex she thought, putting the laptop back on the nightstand. But she couldn't go to sleep without renewing her mind on exactly what God says about love. Opening the top drawer on the nightstand, she pulled out her NIV bible, turned to 1 Corinthians 13:4-8 and read. "Love is patient, love is kind. It does not envy, it does not boast, it is not proud. It does not dishonor others it is not self-seeking, it is not easily angered, it keeps no record of wrongs. Love does not delight in evil but rejoices with the truth. It always protects, always trusts, always hopes, always perseveres. Love never fails...." And with that confirmation, Maria tucked the bible under her comforter, pulling it close to her heart, and drifted off to sleep.

Chapter 11

"Hey Juan, have you seen Ortega this morning? It's 7 am and he's normally here by 6:30 to walk through electrical plans with me on the blueprint", MJ asked while scratching the back of his ear. "No boss, haven't seen him. Me and the crew are down there sorting tools and tidying up the equipment storage room while we wait for him to arrive. I walked back up here hoping to find him myself". "Noted, Juan, thanks. I'll give him a call; in the meantime, keep the guys busy. I'll call you once I touch base with him." MJ's mind immediately thought back to the last place he saw Ortega... Sunday in front of an abandoned building downtown near Reggie's Soul Food.

Chapter 12

"Joe, you missed the excitement at lunch Friday. I had lunch with Dr. Lovertounge." Joe's eyes grew wide when Sierra mentioned Dr. Lovertounge. Sierra had been friends with Joe long enough to read her mind.... and eyes.

"No, no it was just lunch. He didn't ask for my number or offer me out for a dinner date. And it was a quick lunch at that. I was almost done eating when he noticed me and invited himself over. I was quite surprised at the degree to which he was flirting with me." Sierra paused and looked at Joe. "Stop it, Joe," Sierra said while slapping the table, laughing so hard, she almost choked on her Fritos. Joe had yet to say a word while slurping down her tomato soup but the faces she was making had Sierra rolling." If you think that's something, you should know he was glad you were not with me'. Almost choking on her soup Joe's eye now squinted as she mumbled, "what?" "Greg quoted my entire daily schedule, including the fact that I take lunch every day with you... the lady from accounting.... haaaaahaaaaahaaaaa!!!" Sierra was now laughing so hard tears were rolling down her face; she was no longer eating but leaning over the table with her head almost in her lunch bag. Joe's face was so contorted you couldn't tell if she was about to bowl over with laughter or flame up from anger. But Sierra heard her loud and clear when she said, In the most serious voice Sierra had ever heard mumble a syllable, "Blap Blap

Blap, Wraaa, Wraaa,Wraaa, sirens are blaring and I'm the only one hearing them?" "Dr. Lov..., Greg totally crossed the line. He knows you are married. He's married, for goodness sake, and he's flirting with you like neither of you are already committed. I'm offended if you're not. You may think this is funny but all I hear is sirens. Sierra, do not entertain this Dr. Again! And no, not because I want him, but because you have a good thang! Maxwell is a good man and it's no secret that he loves you and your son with all his heart."

Chapter 13

Maria.... Saturday evening, while waiting for the girls to finish playing at the park, she was scrolling through her phone and read an inspirational article that made her spirit leap as she read it.

Give, give, give until there's just no more. Physically exhausted, mentally exhausted. When is your life ever your own? Love is a sacrifice ~ Mae Good Self Reflection Guru.

The article went on to reflect on the Guru's observation of love in relationships from youth until she grew into adulthood. Right or wrong, she'd observed the unspoken love between her parents. It was an uncompromising love. A love she felt that decided if I can't love you up close and personal, then I will love you from afar. As long as she could remember, her parents were intimate people, although sometimes never from within the same house. They broke up and got back together so often that she began to think that was normal. She never heard the argument that got them to the brink of separation but always saw the results. Coming home from school, noticing pieces of furniture missing: a dresser, a T.V., or an entire bedroom set or living room set. The kids remained with Mom. Father would often visit, or they would often visit him. And either visit, time and again, would be overnight. Neither parent ever spoke badly about the other one aloud to any of the kids and, for years, remained married through these breakups. She felt both her parents sacrificed for love, she never concluded if it was for the sake of the family unit or the genuine love, they had for each other.

She also spoke about the love observed between her aunt and uncle; Reece and Joe. They seemed to be married forever though they were middle-aged. The way they related to each other appeared organic, dang near unlearned. From the outside, they were a perfect fit. If you were close enough to them, as the Guru was, you began to learn otherwise. Reece was the author's mother's sister. They were close, like best friends, spending many weekdays and weekends together. Like friends, they were each other's confidants. It was there, sitting within earshot of those conversations, that the author learned that Uncle Joe didn't always talk the nicest to Aunt Reece. Often calling her a man, deceitful, a liar, and sometimes a #itch. They periodically argued about how he felt she was an enabler to their kids, and it would be her fault if they never learned to stand on their own two feet. The author never saw her aunt in that light, yet she also could not conclude that her aunt was not some, all, or none of those things. She also remembered Aunt Reece telling her mom that she knew she needed to love Uncle Joe better. She felt how she loved him was different somehow than what he seemed to need from her. She could clearly see that his love language was words of affirmation and physical touch. Big on encouragement, being appreciated, appreciation shown with action and affirmation, and attention. He also loved to rub her back, for her to sit in his lap or close beside him on the couch. Aunt Reece's love language was acts of service. Showing her affection and love by being an active mother, keeping the house orderly, preparing meals, keeping clothes clean, taking care of things she felt irritated Joe and doing intimate services she knew excited Joe. In all of this it seemed to still not be enough. She had trouble receiving his affection and her acts of service were eventually not enough. What she saw was two people who loved each other but, over time no longer liked each other. They sacrificed for their family and each other.

Lastly, the author concluded the article with a thoughtful question on friendship.

Have you ever looked around and wondered how friendships get to the point of being evasive? Conversations seem forced, interactions become inauthentic, and you'd rather not interact versus fake it. Who has time for that? Life is granted by grace and how dare we take advantage of God's grace by not loving and enjoying life to the fullest. We must always self-evaluate all relationships: marriages, family unions, and friendships. Then make the best decision on how to proceed in those relationships as we grow. Shake that dust off your feet and keep moving toward achieving a fulfilled life.

All Maria could truly think about was that her best friend was abandoning her. Another week had passed. Ortega was home but distant Monday evening through Friday morning. Then bam, no Ortega during the weekend. And when he surfaced on Mondays, he offered no explanation and she demanded none. Sacrificial love...

Chapter 14

Ortega thought he was dreaming, as he lay on the cold floor of the abandoned dilapidated house. He heard the sweetest words...

"Whoa, my love, my darling, I've hungered for your touch, a long, lonely time, and time goes by..... so slowly, and the time can do so much, are you still mine, I need your love, I need your love, I need your love" the singer belted out. The sun demanded to see the pulps of his dark brown eyes. As he succumbed to it, he saw the source of the sound, the old man who was always drunk but never said a word was standing by the window, now, humming the words of "Unchained Melody." Ortega could feel the heaviness of his heart as he sang the verse a second time. His tone was so clear; like he was part of the Motown family, such a stark contrast to the environment he was in.

Pulling himself up on his elbows, Ortega continued to pull himself erect until he was in a sitting position on the floor. He scooted back just a little until his back was against the bottom of the window seal. What a night. It was so grand. Ortega couldn't remember much beyond entering the dilapidated house, finding an unoccupied space on the floor, and sucking on the crystal pipe that held his priority of choice. Now, listening to the fellow prodigal son belt out the words to that beautiful melody he could only think of his family.

"Lonely rivers flow to the sea, to the sea, to the open arms of the sea. Lonely rivers sigh, wait for me, wait for me. I'll be coming home, wait for me." A single tear slowly flowed from his left eye as he wondered how he'd gotten to this point in his life. Why wasn't his family enough to strengthen his ability to fight the urges for this drug? A drug that continued to distort the priority of his heart with the priority of his flesh. He had a family at home 'waiting for him' yet here he was. As his eyes focused on the dilapidation around him and the fellow occupant started the verse of the melody again, Ortega sat and wept.

As he wept his mind thought about his ailing heart and how it always felt unfulfilled. Since he was a young man, he always fantasized about how he would love his wife and how he would then be loved in return the way he desired. He never got the love he wanted as a little boy and thought he would have more control of filling that need as a man only to discover it doesn't work that way. He learned he can't force anyone to love him the way he wants to be loved. Love is a dance, give and take. You give and you get. And you have to be ready to receive the love the way the other person knows to give it. And then be patient as they adapt that love to the way you desire to receive it.

Sometimes that timeframe can be excessive, but the time invested becomes a valuable deposit that makes the wait possible. The love evolves into different types of love as you wait for the desired love. Slowly your heart begins to fill up and you understand how valuable this person and the family you created with this person is in your life.

And it was from this thought that Ortega wept. Thinking about all it was he was going to lose if he stayed on this addictive path. As he slowly came out of his drug-induced state in that dilapidated building, he thought on Psalm 30:2 (NKJV) "O Lord my God I cried out to You and You heard me." Ortega continued to weep.

Chapter 15

Maria finished drying off and continued to pray and talk to God as she began to moisturize with her favorite scent. She was up early, as normal during the work week. Preparing herself, mind, body, and soul, for the day and week ahead. This was her regular morning ritual before waking the kids for school. On this day her heart was heavy thinking about what Ortega could be doing that would keep him from home. Her prayer was really an internal war within her. Physically, she was concerned, but spiritually, she knew only God could address her current situation, the state of her family, and the absence of Ortega. So, this morning, not only did she pray in her natural tongue yet even louder and more vigorous in her spiritual tongue. Maria had no idea what to ask God to fix. She wanted to be specific, so she allowed the Holy Spirit to speak on her behalf, for she trusted His judgment.

"Amen," Maria said aloud as she slid into her shoes, out her bedroom door, and headed to the kitchen to prepare breakfast for the kids. Even though Maria did not work, she wanted to be an example to her girls; always looking and smelling good as a lady should. Pulling out a stack of bowls from the cabinet to prepare oatmeal for the girls, she prepared in silence awaiting instructions for her next move from the Lord. By the time she started preparing the toast, Maria still hadn't received any direction. She began to hum the melody to

CeCe Winans "Never Lost". Stacking the toast on the table she then pivoted to her phone on the cabinet and opened Spotify. Finding the song, she first checked to ensure the phone had a Bluetooth connection to the Bose speaker on top of the fridge. Confirming it was connected she hit play. Walking toward the girls' room to awaken them for school she allowed the lyrics to minister to her.

"You can do all things
You can do all things but fail
'Cause You've never lost a battle
No, You've never lost a battle
And I know, I know
You never will

Everything's possible
By the power of the Holy Ghost
A new wind is blowing right now (oh, yeah)
Breaking my heart of stone
Taking over like it's Jericho
And my walls are all crashing down"

While the girls washed their faces, brushed their teeth, and dressed for school Maria returned to fill the bowls with the warm oatmeal. The song continued in the background, CeCe belting out; "You've never lost a battle (You've never lost a battle) I know, I know You never will". As she filled the last bowl a still sound voice said, call Sierra.

Sirens

Chapter 16

"Have a great day, Max," Sierra yelled as he slammed the car door heading into school. My little boy is growing up, she huffed as she watched him enter the building. She remembered the days when he would yell, by Ma, back. Now-a-days he said nothing. Scurred away from the car and into school like he was running from the plague, never looking back. It could be worse, she thought to herself pulling away from Hines Elementary's pick up and drop off drop zone.

Shifting her focus to the task ahead of her at work, Sierra began to prioritize her to-do list for the day; Mondays were always hectic. New Quad III task always seemed to surface; urgent but not important! She'd promised herself over and over that she would be disciplined and stick to her list. Smiling to herself, discipline was definitely one of the fruits of the spirit she needed more growth in; help me Lord Jesus, she said aloud through her smile.

It was 7:45 am as she turned into the parking lot of West Arizona Hospital – WAH. Not late but not as early as she'd like to have arrived. Most of the staff arrived right at 8 am, so good parking spaces close to the entrance were still available. Her phone rang as she parked in a space one row over from the center row. Putting the car into park and turning the engine off she answered on the third ring, "Hello!"

"Good morning, Sierra. This is Maria. How are you?" "Hi, Maria. I am doing well I hope you are as well." "Not much I can complain about, the girls and I are well. Sorry in advance for calling you so early this morning. However, I wanted to check with you concerning Ortega and MJ." "Oh okay," Sierra said questionably. "Is everything alright?" "I'm not sure," Maria said, "that's why I am calling. For the last two weekends," Maria continued, "Ortega has been MIA. Monday through Thursday he's here with the family after work. Then Friday, he's a no-show, and we don't see him again until Monday night after work again. I was wondering how the business was going? Are there any issues, stressful projects, or side jobs that are keeping Ortega and MJ preoccupied?" Sierra paused and thought for a second. "No, not that I know of. MJ was home the past two weekends. He hadn't mentioned any solo jobs that Ortega was handling but I'm not certain and could check for you." "That would be great, Maria said in an exhaustive breath, that would be great."

Sirens blared internally through Sierra. What is up... she thought to herself. "Ah, you said you were good earlier, but I sense your anxiety concerning Ortega - this seems urgent. Tell you what, let me reach out to MJ right now and get back to you." Maria could only muster a "Thank You" in barely a whisper before hanging up the phone.

Chapter 17

Hanging up the phone, Maria began to reflect on her life and pay attention to the hurt. In her 39 years, she'd taken some shots to the chin and tears on her heart. Nothing seemed to linger like the pain she felt associated with her marriage to Ortega.

Many years ago, her sister Catalina was taken from her abruptly. One day, they were chatting it up laughing on the phone about pie. Specifically, about a sweet potato pie that was being cooked in July. It seemed hilarious at the time. The next day she was gone. Strangled and set on fire by a jealous spouse. Catalina and her beautiful daughter Maya. Both were murdered that day at the hands of Catalina's husband. For months Maria was numb, hesitant to be alone for sheer fear that their memory would be too much to bear alone. Hurt and humbled all at the same time. The heaviest of weights she'd ever bared, the lowest sorrow she'd ever felt. Tears seemed to come from nowhere for months upon months. She could never speak to her sister again. Tried not to be upset with God, knowing that she lost but her sister and niece loss more. So, she pressed on, pressed through the heaviness, through the tears. There were things that needed to be done, a family still here, still needed her. She couldn't just shrivel up and welt away. She had to move forward with a rip on her heart that reshaped it to the point where the silhouette of it would never be the same again.

And like a pierce to the side Maria also endured the loss of her sister/cousin Gabriela, aka Gab. Everyone was devastated when Catalina died. All the cousins grew up close and everyone felt the blow when Catalina and Maya were laid to rest. Maria felt that when she needed Gab the most she completely backed away. Maria would call Gab, and she would seem irritated speaking with her. Maria would keep the conversations short with the intent not to upset Gab, but determined to keep the lines of communication open she continued to reach out. Without any explanation, Gab just stopped talking to her, didn't call, and wouldn't answer her call. She stopped texting and responding to Maria's text. Just stopped. Maria was at a loss; how family could treat someone you say you love that way? She wasn't sure if she was more hurt over the fact that she was being treated like that by someone she thought loved her unconditionally or if it was because of WHO it was treating her like that. Thinking their relationship was more profound, stronger, too important for anything other than death to separate them... Hurt again, Maria couldn't understand how she could lose one sister physically, never able to speak with her again, and lose another, possibly, never speaking to her again. Relationships forever changed. One relationship that could never be rekindled and the other forever damaged. Like a robot, Maria moved on with life. Feeling that she had again missed the siren, warning her that change was inevitable, especially in relationships.

Maria once heard a pastor say, "Your feelings are important, but it is a bad manager". Interpreting that to mean she couldn't go through life making all important decisions based on how she felt. When it came to her marriage, though, she always felt some-type-of-way. Some lingering hurt was always there, and she couldn't figure out what it was that she continued to overlook in her life... in their relationship... that fed that hurt.

Chapter 18

Hello Moto, beep-beep-beep, hello moto. MJ looked down at his ringing phone sitting on his clipboard. He picked this old-school ringtone just for Sierra. It was a distinctive sound, just like her.

He was going over the task for the day with the crew. He always answered his wife's call when he could, handing the clipboard to Juan, MJ asked him to complete the overview with the crew.

"Hi babe!"

"Hi, MJ, sorry to bother you so early. I know you're probably preparing your crew for the day."

"You know my routine well babe. What's going on, you rarely call me in the AM, do I have an appointment later today or something?"

"No, not today. I had a call this morning from Maria, which was abnormal. We do talk from time to time but not often on the phone. She sounded very concerned MJ about Ortega. He's not coming home during the weekend."

Turning around in a circle, near the entrance to the site, MJ repeated Sierra's last statement, "he's not coming home during the weekend?"

"Exactly," Sierra responded. "I told her I would check with you to see if he was on a special weekend assignment for work or if you had any insight into what he may be up to."

Stopping and looking toward the parking lot, MJ noticed Ortega getting out of his navy-blue Malibu. A heaviness dropped in MJ's spirit as he observed his old friend stroll his way. He wore the same clothes he had on Friday; khaki carpenter pants with dark mud stains on the right knee and the lime green t-shirt with a yellow graphic hard hat printed on the right sleeve. Not only were they still dirty from work completed on Friday, but the closer he got to him, he could see that shirt also now looked like it was covered in soot.

"No and no," MJ said softly into the phone, as he held his palm up to Ortega and mouthed for him to hold on, no weekend work assignments and no insight on what's going on. Turning his back to Ortega, he finished up his call with Sierra. Ending with, "I'll talk to you later babe," as he clicked the red phone icon and slid the phone into his pocket.

"Hey man, I was just about to go get coffee. That's why I stopped you, would you like a cup, it's on me?"

MJ observed Ortegas face change from dejection to perky.

"Yes," Ortega responded.

MJ said nothing more, smiled and pointed toward the breakfast food truck parked to the left of the construction entrance. They walked to the truck in silence. Arriving at the truck, MJ ordered a small decaf with 3 creams and 1 Splenda. "Add whatever he wants", stepping to the side so the attendant could take Ortega's coffee order as well. MJ took the few seconds to pray, asking God to direct his words, to give him wisdom and insight on what to say and how to say it.

"MJ," Ortega said in a low tone, "thanks for the coffee it's just what I need this morning. And thanks for not tearing into me for being late. I ah, I ah had a rough start this morning and then couldn't find my keys." Smiling wearily and taking a slow sip of black caffeinated coffee, he looked at MJ over the rim of his cup awaiting a reply. All he got was a pat on the back and a warm smile.

MJ didn't feel any nudging from God to address anything further. So, he said, 'It happens to the best of us, even top dogs ... Old Yeller," ... they looked at each other and cracked up laughing. Breaking the ice and shifting the atmosphere. "Alright, man, not sure what's troubling you but know that I'm here for you. Meet me here at 11:30 for lunch, my treat, I have something I'd like to share with you." Stopping mid-stride, MJ looked at Ortega and said "Deal?" "Deal," Ortega said.

"My man" MJ said as they both headed back into the site to get to work.

Maxwell Construction was leaving its mark in Opng Arizona, just north of Flagstaff. The current project was the start of a much-needed recreational district in what will become an extension of downtown. From the city plans MJ was privy to Opng had plans for Main Event family game center, Babe Ruth batting, indoor soccer fields, and basketball courts and a huge Top Golf facility. MJ's company won the bid to complete all electrical for Top Golf. The town is excited to finally have family entertainment eliminating the need to drive to surrounding cities on the weekends. This should be a significant revenue driver for the city; more local dollars invested and increased spending from citizens in smaller surrounding towns who will most definitely start to make Opng their entertainment city of choice.

The town decided to start with Top Golf first, knowing that its well-known name would be an immediate draw. As MJ reviewed drawings validating the specifications for the back right side of the foundation, he began to wonder what he would share with Ortega. In 3 hours, it will be lunchtime. Surely something was going on with him. MJ was not the kind of man to make assumptions about people; if he could help it, given the opportunity, he addressed things head-on. Taking in Ortega this morning, he could see his friend was struggling with something. Couple that with the fact that he was sure it was Ortega in front of the abandoned building downtown Sunday evening. He was either picking up prostitutes or looking for drugs. Neither were activities he wanted to see his friend lose everything over; both addictive habits. And just like that God nudged him and dropped in his spirit precisely what to share with Ortega during lunch.

'Thank you, God,' MJ said aloud as he reeled back in his measuring tape and jotted the numbers down on the pocket pad. As he continued to work, he continued to thank God for various things in his life; family, health, soundness, favor, grace, provision, friends.... he could go on and on. And he did, naming any and everything he could think about for the next 30 minutes as he worked. 'Beep... MJ', looking down at his belt loop MJ, unclipped the job-site walkie-talkie. Even with the popularity of smartphones, MJ stuck with the old-school, dependable walkie-talkies for his job sites. "Yes," he said. "Can you come over to the west side to the power connection box? We need you to confirm the installation to assure we are proceeding to install this thing to code." "On my way Jus," MJ said, "headed in that direction."

It was 11:25 am when MJ and Jus completed the walkthrough. Just enough time for MJ to wash up and head out to meet Ortega at the food truck for lunch. Washing his hands, he thought of one of his favorite scriptures Galatians 6: 1-2; "1 Brothers and sisters, if someone is caught in a sin, you who live by the Spirit should restore that person gently. But watch yourselves, or you also may be tempted. 2 Carry each other's burdens, and in this way, you will fulfill the law of Christ." And that's just what he would do.

Chapter 19

"Slaw dog, only mustard with a bag of plain Lays and a Dr. Pepper please." MJ could already taste the mustard in the homemade slaw Moma Nea whipped up daily for patrons of Nea's Good Cooking food truck. Nishnea Bianco, is a little Italian lady from Nevada who moved to northern Arizona to take care of her ailing sister five years ago. A retired home economics teacher, with no husband or kids of her own, had nothing remaining in Nevada to keep her there. From the great state of New York, Nishnea and her sister moved west after graduating from Stony Brook University with bachelor's in education. Determined to start work soon after graduation, they both registered with Midwest Teacher & Administrator Placement Agency, which placed Nishnea in Henderson, Nevada, and her sister Gianna in Opng, Arizona.

Nishnea was an amazing cook. During her time away from taking care of Gianna she would go downtown to the community youth center and cook an after-school meal for the kids once a week. They absolutely loved to see Nishnea coming, pulling her purple utility wagon full of groceries for that day's supper. She had a big heart and a calling to serve youth. She quickly became known as Moma Nea at the center. After being in Opng 11 months, caring for her sister and serving the youth Nishnea settled into her new surroundings. The town had grown on her. She'd wished different circumstances directed her here yet grateful to God that at her age she was able to still be of service to her sister and Gods little ones.

Gianna succumbed to her illness a week before Thanksgiving. Heartbroken that she didn't make the full recovery she so desperately prayed for, Nishnea still held onto Gods word. Her sister was her best friend, losing her was just as heavy as losing her mom ten years ago. She and Gianna mourned the loss of their mom together and now she had to grieve this loss alone. Nishnea believed every written word God left us in His word. Drawing her strength from 2 Corinthians 5:8 (NIV) & Isaiah 61:3 (NKJV)...

2 Corinthians 5:8 "we are confident, yes, well pleased rather to be absent from the body and to be present with the Lord"

Isaiah 61:2-3, "2.... to comfort all who mourn 3, to console those who mourn in Zion, to give them beauty for ashes, The oil of joy for mourning, The garment of praise for the spirit of heaviness; ..."

Believing that her sister had endured her sickness a long time, if God didn't see fit for her to stay here on earth, then with him was a much better option. And she took comfort in knowing that God saw her in her grief and was there with her through it all.

Cooking became her safehouse through it all. In her purpose lay the healing she needed to keep going. The community center was constrained on the number of hours she could volunteer per month. God then laid it on her heart to invest in a food truck; giving her the freedom to cook when she wanted and for who she wanted. She always heard the little ones in the community center mess hall chatting away while they were waiting to eat, and she often heard the regulars tell the newbies; "just wait, it's going to be good because Moma Nea got some good cooking". Hearing that made her heart smile. So, she transferred that good feeling to her food truck, calling it Moma Neas Good Cooking. Four years later she still serves breakfast and lunch at work sites like the one she's at today. The proceeds are then used to purchase groceries for the additional free meals she provides during the week for the little ones and anyone else who needed a good hot meal, in the community center parking lot. When God sees a will, He always makes a way!

"One slaw dog combo coming up," Moma Nea said to MJ with a smile. "And for you?", she said, looking past MJ at Ortega. Looking at her, he hesitated slightly, then ordered the same combo but added onions and subbed Dr. Pepper for a Coke. Smiling, she turned around and gave the short-order cook, standing two steps to her left, the order to prepare. As MJ paid, she announced the order would be ready in a jiffy. They stepped to the side to wait while Moma Nea continued to take orders. "116", she yelled out a few minutes later. Looking at his receipt MJ headed to the food truck window to pick up their order. As MJ loaded the two can sodas in his cargo pants pockets to free his hands to carry the two cardboard trays housing their slaw dogs, Moma Nea took the opportunity to share her concern.

"Young man," she said softly, "I've served your friend during the Free Fry Day Meals I provide Saturday evenings in the parking lot of the community youth center downtown. I'm not selective of who I serve but I am observant. Know that he may need your prayers and support more than you'd ever know. At God's nudging keep pouring into him with kindness and understanding because addiction is real."

"Yes mam", MJ said with a nod. "Here you go man. Some of the best slaw dogs in the area. Moma Nea makes the best homemade slaw I've ever tasted." "Thanks again MJ. I feel like I haven't eaten in days," Ortega said while seemingly devouring his slaw dog in 3 bites. The city built a good size covered shelter with multiple picnic tables and trash cans near the entrance of the construction site. MJ and Ortega were solo at one of the tables finishing up their lunch. Thinking about the comment from Moma Nea and the earlier nudging from God, MJ felt it was no better time than the present to share a testimony with Ortega.

"Remember this morning at breakfast, I mentioned I wanted to share something with you later?" Ortega nodded while sipping his Coke. "About 10 years ago when I was younger, much younger, and me and Sierra were in the early parts of our marriage. I was really struggling with intimacy, and it made me sometimes feel worthless. I absolutely adored my baby and had no problem in the sex department, but the intimacy was missing. We..., I... was disconnected when it came to intimacy because I saw it as sex while Sierra saw intimacy as sacrifice and sharing. The lack of intimacy was beginning to cause ripples in my marriage. I began to feel a sense of resentment from Sierra when I needed her intimately." Rubbing his hands together as if putting on lotion, to wipe the dew from the Dr. Pepper off his hands, MJ looked at Ortega with a dubious smile, "You look like you're saying where is this coming from and where is he going with it? Yes, I'ma get to my point," MJ said.

"Porn. Pornography, that is. I was addicted." Ortega sat with a flabbergasted look on his face. "Yeah", MJ said. "Newly married to the love of my life, saved... a Christian with a relationship with God. He-God and I spoke all the time, but man, I was addicted to porn. What started as a stopgap to fill a desire so I wouldn't have sex outside of marriage turned into a vice to fill the desires of my flesh even after my marriage. Instead of speaking to God about my fleshly desires, I made a bad battle worse by using porn to self-gratify myself. How deceptive I allowed my mind to be, telling myself that watching porn was better than having sex before marriage. The right answer was to deny myself altogether. No matter how natural it was for me to have those feelings, I should have denied those feelings altogether and chased after God like my life depended on it. Because it did. The things I saw looking at porn, the bodies, positions, and acts planted a seed in me, making my flesh crave the physical response porn gave me all–the-time! It became a thing requiring no connection, no intimacy as long as I got a physical response. It took a lot for me to admit I was addicted to porn. I didn't feel like I was hurting anyone, at first. Then, after watching it, I started feeling worthless every time the high passed. Sierra never found out how much I was looking at porn, but she did notice a change when I finally got free from it. When Sierra started to explain to me what she meant by 'missing intimacy,' I started trying to identify other things in my life that I just received a reaction from but had no connection to. It was like a siren going off, loud and deafening. Yet crippling. Crippling to my marriage. So, I reached out to Bishop Give. Told him what I was struggling with and that I need guidance, help overcoming what seemed to physically pull on my flesh and appear difficult not to act when I thought about it. We prayed and fasted together, but the biggest help for me was having Bishop Give talk this out with me. He 'was' a safe place, non-judging, cared about me, and didn't turn his nose up because of what I was struggling with. I meet with him on a weekly basis for months. And anytime I had a moment of weakness he was always a phone call away to help me work through those times as well, until my flesh strengthened, and the feeling of worthlessness went away."

"Letting go of my porn addiction allowed me to pick up intimacy. I understood what Sierra was communicating and began to exhibit it in our relationship. She never knew it was because I gave up the addiction. One that I am still very conscious of today. It attempts to rear its head from time to time. I am in a different space, though, mentally, physically, and mostly, spiritually. I had to chase God harder and discipline myself to always listen to the holy spirit nudging me when I may put myself in a place of exposure, but I'm free. I have God to thank for that. God gave me the choice to choose me, then He helped me work to overcome my flesh and reminded me that I have the Holy Spirit as a keeper!"

"I just want to let you know man, that whatever you're going through, I'm a safe place."

Chapter 20

I'm a safe place. I'm a safe place. Ortego thought about the last thing MJ said to him today. Psalm 46:1 came rushing back to him;

"God is our refuge and strength, an ever-present help in trouble."

Definitely, in trouble, he thought... feeling beyond addiction, beyond help, beyond God's saving grace. He himself felt disgraced. He felt weak-minded, mad at himself for not being strong enough to dig himself out of this hole he allowed himself to fall into. God has been so good to me he thought. And I betrayed him, thinking I'm in control. He felt like punching something. Balling up his fist he struck the dashboard of his car. And again, and again and again, until he yelled, "Ahhhhh!"

Still, sitting in his car, parked on site, yet to leave work. Not sure where he was headed. Knowing he needed to go home and check on his family, he dreaded going. He dreaded having to face the people he loved most. Knowing he messed up, feeling the disappointment he expected they would have, from the people he looked to satisfy the most.

Four beautiful daughters who depend on me and a loving wife who trusts, depends on, and never betrayed me. God has given me gifts more precious than jewels, and I'm handling them like oil greased mechanic rags. He sat and cried.

Ortega cried warm streams of silent tears until his vision became blurry and his eyes began to burn.

He was just sooo mad at himself for turning away from God for a few minutes to fellowship with guys at the hotel in New Mexico who were also in the area working on a construction project. He had a long day at work that day. Getting back to the hotel, he showered and left the room intending to ride out to the nearest restaurant for dinner. MJ was under the weather and decided to pass up dinner in exchange for an early night of rest intending to beat off the oncoming sickness. They were there on assignment, now was not the time to get sick and miss work. So, Ortega headed out alone. Finding the nearest Chinese buffet, he ordered a General Tso Chicken entrée with spring rolls, to go. Arriving back at the hotel he turned on the radio and ate his dinner in the work truck. Looking around the parking lot, he noticed other traveling tradesmen seemed to be doing the same thing; sitting and eating. No doubt, resting and preparing for the next day. They were probably missing their families as he was, but were also committed to doing the necessary to provide for them. It was nearing 9 pm, "I better get back and turn in, these 5 am mornings are kicking my tail". Opening the truck door, he almost hit the vehicle door of the truck backed in beside him. The occupant was also exiting. "Sorry man", Ortega said, smelling a strong scent of weed. "It's all good," the tradesman said exiting his truck. "And it's about to get even better, we were just about to visit with Mary Jane, daa daa," he said with a little chuckle. "She always gets us right for the next workday, making these long weeks easier to bare." The tradesman fist-bumped his partner near the hood of the truck while smiling at Ortega and holding up the blunt. Ortega, standing in the open driver-side door of his truck, shook his head left to right and said, "Nah man, I'm good!" "Suit yourself," the tradesman uttered with a flip of his wrist as if he was shooing away a fly, "she never disappoints!"

Thinking to himself; he'd not smoked a blunt since his high school graduation after party. Remembering the party, the school held for all graduating seniors at the civic center near the school in New Mexico. He and all his automotive shop class buddies had snuck out the back door near the civic center kitchen to smoke a little herb. They often got together after school to smoke. One of his classmates had an older brother who lived in their basement and was a weed-head. The basement had an access point where the brother, on many occasions, sat and smoked at night leaving unfinished buds in a tin can hidden on the inside of an old tire that leaned against the back of the house. His classmate oftentimes grabbed a few unfinished buds for them. The bud was never any longer or wider than a dime, just enough for five shop class nerds to take a puff and pass around twice.

They had no time after school today since today was graduation. So, they all agreed to meet up at the graduation party. This would be their last puff giggle session. All were headed in different directions after graduation; some to four-year colleges to study technology and education, some to trade school to study electrical and HVAC, and one decided to head to the Navy to serve our country, specializing in logistics. All wise enough to know weed could derail their plans so vowed this was it! Entering back through the kitchen of the civic center, they finished up the night munching on party snacks, graduation cake, dancing to Montell Jordans "This Is How We Do It" and Reel 2 Real's "I Like to Move It." Feeling happy and excited about their accomplishment and expectant future.

Remembering those content times compared to how lonely and tired he felt now, Ortega entertained the tradesman's offer. It's just a little weed, he thought. "**No**", an inner voice said. "**That's old flesh, that's not who you are today... in Christ**", the voice said. Again, his thoughts went back to how he used to feel with his shop buddies. "**Danger,**" the voice said again. Ignoring the voice Ortega said, "weed is not harmful, and it will help me sleep well" to himself. Looking toward the entrance of the hotel he saw the tradesman leaning against the wall with his partner, "Yo compadre", he yelled out. Clicking the key fob and locking the truck doors he walked toward him. "Si, si, amigo," the tradesman said with a heavy slur. He must be liquoring up with that weed, Ortega thought, he already looked done for the night. "I changed my mind; let me get one puff." The tradesman looked back at his partner and then back at Ortega. "Amigo," he said slowly, "the bite on this Mary Jane may be too much for you. I was only being polite earlier man. Catch me tomorrow and I'll have some with less kick." **"Go,"** the voice said to Ortega. "Manana", Ortega repeated. "Manana," the tradesman said with a thumbs up. Walking away, Ortega wrestling with the voice telling him to go and his flesh telling him to go back, it's harmless, remember your high school days and how tired you are now. He stopped one step from the hotel entrance. Turning around towards the tradesman, he asked once more, "Just one puff? I can handle it." Staring at Ortega for about five seconds, the tradesman handed Ortega the Mary Jane, "It's your choice."

Waking up the next morning, Ortega had no memory of entering his room or getting in bed. Sitting up and looking down at his feet he realized he still had his shoes on. The only thing he remembered was feeling a high that was so otherworldly just seconds after taking that puff. He'd never felt anything like it. It was nothing like the buds he'd experienced in high school. All day long, all he could think about was last night's high. After work, he found the tradesman and questioned him about the type of weed, he smoked, only to find out that his Mary Jane was weed laced with crack!

And since the first New Mexico trip, Ortega has been fighting the urge for the drug alone. Often losing the battle. "I need help!" he cried. Thinking about MJ's comment again...

I'm a safe place. Ortega decided to take MJ up on his offer and share his struggle.

When. He wasn't sure when, but he now felt he could, when he was ready.

Chapter 21

"Girls," Maria yelled as she was finishing up the dishes from tonight's dinner. "Yes, ma," four little voices replied. "it's time to get your baths and prepare for school tomorrow."

Maria and Ortega produced four beautiful girls. Alandra is the oldest, twelve years old, and in the 6th grade. She is almost a spitting image of Ortega with her boxy frame, full face, and long thick, jet-black hair. Next is Liliana. Ana, as her mom calls her, is ten years old in the 4th grade. She loves all things related to Social Studies and can quote all 50 states in alphabetical order. Ana resembles Maria's fair-skinned grandmother with wavy, almost auburn-colored hair. The caretaker of the bunch is Carmen. At only seven years old she always makes sure all her sisters have what they need. Carmen, a 2nd grader, looked the most like Maria with curly hair and the makings of what already looked like an athletic build. Rounding out the crew is Isabella. Her older sisters call her Bella and her dad, who is the apple of her eye, calls her Izzy. Isabella is the pulse of the Ortega home. At four years old and only in pre–K you would think she has been on earth before. She says many things laced with wisdom, which is hysterical sometimes coming from a four-year-old. Bella rarely says anything at a normal decibel, and of course, she is the one Maria hears the clearest when the argument starts between the girls about who would take their bath first.

"Stop the back-and-forth girls. Why do we always have to go through this?" Maria asked. "Alandra, take your bath first, then help Bella with her bath and clothes for tomorrow. Then, Ana, you're next, then Carmen." "Yes, ma," they all said in unison.

For the next 45 minutes, all Maria heard upstairs was running water filling the bathtub, drawers slamming, and little feet running around. Bella, she thought, for sure was the culprit making all the noise. That little girl never does anything quietly. Just like her dad, Maria smiled. Then, almost immediately the giddy feeling faded, and she began to be filled with a feeling of anxiety and sadness. It was almost 7:30 pm and Ortega still hadn't shown his face. She knew from the call with Sierra this afternoon that he did make it to work today. And per MJ, they were not working on any unusually stressful projects. MJ had agreed to investigate deeper considering he was also concerned about the unusual behavior he'd observed as well. Sierra didn't elaborate any further than that but promised she would be in touch if MJ said more.

Just as she finished wiping down the kitchen counters and sweeping the floor, she heard keys to the front door rattling.

The girls are still up, Ortega guessed, leaning forward looking at the upstairs lights through his windshield. He pulled into the driveway five minutes ago but had yet mustered up the courage to go inside. Checking the clock on the car radio it was only 7:25 pm. Late but not late enough for them to be in bed, he thought. Still feeling a little anxious he wasn't quite sure what he wanted to do. He'd stopped by the boarding house after work. Even after the conversation with MJ and coming to the realization that he needed help fighting this addiction, he gave in to his flesh and smoked the cryptic poison once more. Ortega felt the war within himself. His mind and heart told him to fight to be free of this drug and be a present husband and dad to his family. While his body craved the drug and reverberated for it like a sound wave moving from the top of his head to the tip of his toes. Wanting to pray but at the same time feeling unworthy and ashamed to even speak to God, he made the decision to go in the house and face the people he'd been dreading having to confront all day. Feeling so lost but present, his insides felt like a top spinning out of control as he walked up the driveway towards the house. And just like a top, he felt like he was spinning at an unsafe speed, trying to keep his balance at the edge of it all. As if he was about to topple over, but the speed of it all kept him from falling. And just like the top he felt he was designed to withstand it all, but his mind couldn't see how.

Reaching for the front door, he heard Izzy scream, "I'm telling Mom." Stepping around his apprehension Ortega unlocked the door and went inside.

His first encounter was with Maria. As he closed the door and turned around, their eyes met.

Maria was still holding the broom and he his keys as they held each other's gaze. Both were locked in, saying with their eyes things their mouth had yet interrupted.

Maria stood and looked at me for just a second with the emptiest expression before fake smiling and telling me, "Hi." I could see the hurt and the determination not to allow it to prevail. She put the broom away in the laundry room near the back door on the other side of the kitchen. "Are you hungry?" she said, as I unglued myself from the spot I was stuck to and headed to her in the kitchen. "I'm sure the food is still warm. I'd just put it away while the girls are getting their baths." I took a seat at the island behind her as she prepared my food. Looking around the house, things were so orderly and clean. Not sterile clean but relaxed comfortable clean. And it smelled so wonderful. Undoubtedly, Maria made their house a home, he thought. Oh, my goodness, he almost said aloud, when she turned around with a big bowl of Posole. Chicken soup, Posole style was like a welcome home meal he felt he didn't deserve. Tender chicken, hominy, chili peppers, cumin, oregano, shredded cabbage with a dollop of avocado. As sirens blared in his head, reminding him of all he stood to lose if he didn't get free of this addiction, he quickly closed his eyes, blessed his food, and thanked God for grace. As he started devouring the Posole the microwave beeped. Maria then placed 3 cinnamon sugar churro bites and a glass of milk near his bowl. Pausing slightly to look at her he couldn't help but smile. He smiled because he felt so loved.

How could he, she thought, while placing the churro bites on the island beside Ortega? Feeling the plastered smile on her face and pure rage churning around her heart, she couldn't understand how he could sit there in the same dingy clothes he left wearing days ago, eating the meal she'd prepared for her girls and smile!

Cooking was her passion, falling behind a love for God and family. It was her love language for those she cared so deeply for. On the way home from school today she heard the girls talking about how much they missed their daddy and hoped that he would be back from 'work' soon. Knowing the truth, all she could think was to ensure that they felt loved, even more than usual when they got home. A hearty meal would have to be the prescription tonight. Remembering back to her childhood, Posole always made her feel so loved at her abuela house. And it was indeed a labor of love to prepare it. Arriving home, Maria checked the girls' homework folders, intending to get them started on their homework before heading off to begin dinner. To her surprise, only Alandra had a homework assignment. Write your spelling words in ABC order and write them three times each – due Tuesday, the homework assignment read. "Okay, little momma, get to writing", Maria said to Alandra as she gently tapped her on the noise. "You three musketeers, come with me." Following Maria to the kitchen in a giddy gallop the girls anticipated the fun that awaited. Giving them all assignments with final instructions to meet at the kitchen island. "Bella, grab the chopping board from the laundry room closet. Carman, get the spices: cumin, oregano, garlic powder, salt, pepper, and a can of hominy from the cabinet. Ana, I need cabbage, peppers, and avocado from the fridge." Maria then began to unpack and wash the chicken breast she'd taken out of the freezer this morning and placed in the sink to thaw. Somehow, between their assignment routes and final island destination, they all arrived back adorned with aprons that read 'Tiny Chef'. Turning around to the island, with the chicken breast now in a pan, ready to season it. Maria couldn't help but smile at her tiny chefs. Not certain where her mom found those cute little colorful aprons, in four different beautiful vibrant colors, but she was sure happy the girls loved to wear them while assisting her in the kitchen.

For the next thirty minutes, they stood around the island chatting it up while helping Maria season, chop, pit, peel, and wrap dinner for the night. Learning, bonding, and making memories, and Maria hoped in an atmosphere that felt filled with love together with food that she shed her motherly love into. She felt lacking in some areas of her life but loving her family through food was not one of them. She also had a surprise for the girls that would go perfect with her Posole, bite size cinnamon sugar churro's, she made while they were away at school.

Looking at Ortega sitting there smiling while eating the churro bites, she saw her oldest baby's face, Alondra. Alondra had the same response eating the churros after dinner. However, Maria adored that she had that response to her food. It was just the response she was hoping for. In that instant she felt the Holy Spirit untangling her heart from the rage she felt minutes earlier. Reminding her of 1 Corinthians 13:5 & 7 (NLT)

"Love... is neither rude. It does not demand its own way. It is not irritable, and it keeps no record of being wronged. 13:7 love never gives up, never loses faith, is always hopeful and endures through every circumstance."

"Ortega, this can't continue. We have to talk."

Chapter 22

With a mouth full of churros all Ortega could do was stare at her in silence. He was not ready to have this conversation with Maria.

It was the middle of the week. This was the exact reason he avoided coming home. He was already a disgrace to himself; he already knew she too would be disgraced with him once she knew what was going on and that Ortega could not take right now.

"I agree", he finally said. "We need to talk, but right now I need to shower and sleep. I know things have been weird, but if we can hold this conversation until the weekend, I promise I will tell you what's going on. I just can't talk about it right now Maria."

Getting up from the island, he rinsed his hands in the sink, removing the cinnamon crystals he accumulated from the churros. Dried them off and headed for their bedroom.

The entire time, Maria stood with her arms folded looking at him. In that instant, the love she felt for him just moments ago began to turn like an evening wave violently crashing against a beach shore attempting to roll across her heart like hate. Instantly the holy spirit dropped Mark 4:39 (KJV) in her spirit; "And He arose, and rebuked the wind, and said unto the sea, peace be still. And the wind ceased, and there was a great calm."

Hate could not keep her heart imprisoned. Like a receding wave that crashed ashore, the wave of hate washed away and was replaced again with love. Confusion, too, yet love resided. Maria took a seat at the kitchen island. Hurt radiating through her chest, and she whispered, "God ,please help us."

The next thing she knew Ortega was coming out of the room with a bag of clothes in his hand. As he walked toward her, she assumed he changed his mind about sleep and a shower. He seemed to be leaving.

Walking toward her, he stopped in front of her, "It's no one else but you Maria. I love you and God is going to help me, help us! I can't disappoint you anymore tonight and don't want to startle the girls." Maria looked shocked but did not say a word. He continued, "I promise we will talk this weekend." Pivoting, he walked toward the door and left.

Hurt, tears streaming down his face, and now with a strong urge for a hit to release him from this pain he left his home and drove off toward downtown.

Chapter 23

Tom Black was a god sent.

Working for him was just the ministry Sierra needed after working under the notorious J. W. Powers. That man was a sly, cynical, brass absolute workplace bully. You would think he was on the school playground the way he attempted to pit one employee against the other. A war of favorites; a few coworkers played the game, but most didn't. The goal of the game was to see who would stick the closest, agree with everything, laugh the hardest, and do the most tasks to gain J.W.'s favor. If you got anywhere near J. W. you could cut the nepotism with a knife. And those who played his game banked on it to gain preference during promotions, senior-level job opportunities, and to avoid the work no one really wanted to do.

Sierra had never worked for such an insecure, power-seeking, good o boy in her entire career.

She'd had stern, demanding managers before, but they were always fair. No intimidation, only an expectation of responsibility and accountability. Characteristics easily respectable in an employee – employer relationship.

Those who did not play the game often felt the wrath of J.W. Powers. Sierra, of course, did not play the game.

Noncompliance, to the nonplayer specific rules, almost destroyed Sierra's career. If you didn't play the war of favorites you were expected to keep silent, ignore the obvious and look the other way; nonplayer rules. Mostly all J. W.'s employees who did not play that game did just that because they feared him and the thought of losing their job. Sierra was one who initially chose to look the other way. When the circumstances didn't include her that is. She had no desire to be close to J.W. Nor desired to be in his amen corner, laughing and agreeing with every word that dripped from his lips. She felt promotions were regulated by human resources and merit based on performance reviews and she had no desire for a senior level position. Seeing no benefit in playing his game, she aligned with the position's work schedule, worked hard and efficiently with her direct internal and external customers, and simply took care of her work responsibilities.

Initially, she looked the other way until the biased culture directly impacted her, more specifically her career record.

A damaged front tire on her black Honda Accord Sport required a trip to the tire shop. Knowing that it was closing in on time to replace all tires she scheduled for all 4 tires to be replaced. Instead of taking a vacation day for the 2-hour round trip appointment, she decided to start work early and work to her normal schedule to fulfill the required 8-hour workday as she had many times before. And frankly, everyone in the department had. J. W. never had an issue with his employees making up time before, but Sierra was made an example of.

Arriving in the office at 7 am and leaving for the tire shop at 8 am, the day started otherwise uneventful. The shop was 15 minutes down the road and the appointment was at 8:30 am. Arriving before time, the Tech had her car registered and on the risers by 8:30. Forty-five minutes later she was on her way back to the office of Scroll Compressors by Brown where she was a commodity manager for Sheet Metal. It was exactly 9:30 am when she entered the automatic doors of the building. Singing a good morning to Gail the building security/front entrance attendant, as she badged into the security door leading to the Purchasing department offices. By 9:35 she was logging back into the office Network to get back to work. By noon, Sierra was pecking away at the keyboard, heavily submerged into a component analysis that was on her 'to be completed by month end list'. The day so far had been productive. Working through her lunch hour as she'd planned to do to complete making up for the two hours she lost taking her car to the shop that morning, Sierra was pleased with how much she had accomplished so far that day. At 12:45 an HR admin was in her cubicle asking if she had a few minutes to join him in his office. Taken aback, she could not imagine what the impromptu visit and invitation was all about. Fifteen minutes later, she was headed back to her cubicle completely stunned and flabbergasted. She worked the rest of the day in a fog, saying much of nothing to anyone except during phone calls with suppliers following up on leads and resolving issues associated with her commodity portfolio.

It wasn't until after dinner that night that she actually let the events of the day out like a hot air balloon. She and MJ were washing dishes after dinner. Max was a toddler at the time, who had already been bathed and tucked into bed.

"You haven't said much tonight, Sierra, other than you had a very eventful day. Any issues with the Techs at the time shop today?" "No, not at all. The appointment went smoothly, and there were no surprises or additional costs."

Silence.

MJ rinsed and dried a few more dishes before asking more specific questions about her day at the office. "How is the quote analysis going for the new large scroll compressor units? Any pushback from J.W.?"

Like a match light to a firecracker, Sierra didn't seem to even take a breath before unloading the events of the day. "After having a seat in John's office, he proceeded to ask me how I was. Fine, I said, probably with a lot of sauce in my response because, at this point, I am on edge, wondering why I'm even in the HR office. He proceeds to tell me he is conducting an investigation on the merits of a complaint that was filed against me on stealing time."

"Stealing time," MJ repeated with a frown and look of shock on his face. "Exactly," Sierra said in a volume louder than she spoke in before. Taking the dish dry off towel from

MJ's shoulder and while drying her hands off she feels MJ in on all the details of the complaint.

John proceeds to tell Sierra that J. W. emailed him a concern that she was stealing time. Even today she was seen coming in late. Communicating that my Outlook calendar was blacked out this morning for two hours as if I had an internal meeting, but I wasn't even in the office. J. W. stated in his email, "he knows this because he stopped by your cube this morning to ask a question, but you were not there. He also checked with your coworkers, which no one had seen you or knew your whereabouts either."

"And what was your reply," MJ asked, as he leaned back against the counter with his arms folded across his chest.

"I told John my whereabouts and tire appointment. I told him that it's common practice in our department to make up with additional work any hours missed because of personal appointments as long as it does not impact anything of importance in the office. I told him I'd done the same before and so have others in my department, and no one has ever been accused of stealing time. I mentioned, as you can see, I was sitting at my desk working during my lunch hour and that I had started at 7 am this morning, 2 hours worked for the 2-hour appointment when I was outside of the office. I directed him to check the badge reader records since he didn't believe me. We don't punch a clock to record our time, but that badge reader records all time in, and that he would find I badged in at 7 am and again at 9:30 am. Time arrived this morning and time returned from my appointment. He told me he would investigate the badge reader, he'd not thought to check it, but for now, he was letting me know it was a serious accusation, they would be investigating this further, and that the account would be in my records until."

"Until," MJ said bewildered now himself. "What in the high heavens does he mean by until?"

Shaking her head Sierra mumbled, "I guess until they find proof that contradicts the accusation."

Silence.

They both stood there in silence for what seemed like minutes but were actually only seconds, staring at each other. Both bridling their tongue, both cautious of the life their words could give this event.

MJ then grabbed Sierra's hands, pulled her in close, and hugged her tightly. Then, pushing her away, he grabbed her hands again in his, as if covering hers, and prayed. "God of all order, ruler of all, we thank You for this day. Thank you for the breath we have in our body, life, health, and strength. We thank you for being all and knowing all. We thank you for telling us in your word that where we are weak You are yet strong. God, in this situation, we do not understand why something that was so common has come against Sierra as an uncommon incident. Still, we know and trust that You do, and because You do we trust that You've already resolved this situation. We ask that You give us Your thoughts, words, and actions as we move through this situation. Guide us oh Lord, like only you can. In Jesus name we pray. Amen."

And that was how they went through that difficult time, with much prayer. MJ and Sierra prayed through the investigation, prayed through the wait, prayed after receiving the results of the findings, and prayed to God to show them what Sierra's next career move should be. Surely after all the wretchedness slithering in this place, God didn't intend for her to remain under the leadership of J.W. Powers any longer.

HR found nothing. The badge reader supported Sierra's explanation of her arrival and departure that day. The accusation was dropped but remnants of the investigation remained in her work file. And that, too, was unsettling to Sierra who felt like she did absolutely nothing to get hooked into one of J.W.'s office games.

Years later, working under Tom Black, she still thanked God for blessing her with a boss full of integrity and a healthy dose of emotional intelligence. She couldn't help but be reminded daily that God knows exactly what we need.

And here is where Sierra's troubles set. She could not mentally let go of the fact that an investigation into stealing time still existed in her work records.

She was no longer with that company or working for J.W. but it irked her that the history of that event lingered. It bothered her even more that she was ever accused of such a thing. A deed so far beneath her character that she still carried the shame of the accusation even though she was found innocent. It was completely out of her control and not impacting her at all, but some things Sierra let mentally irritate her. The thought itself was rubbing her thoughts raw as if she was wearing a burlap potato sack with no underclothes on. She could count the number of people who knew about the situation on one hand, but still, her thoughts constantly spoke to her. She told her she wasn't good enough for anything set in front of her. She said that she was a fraud and that people would eventually find out she could not deliver on those tasks expected of her. And constantly whispered, you landed the job but how long before they fire you for all your inadequacies!

Knowing for a fact the accusation that took place and how the events unfolded were out of her control, yet it was still a mental battle. So insignificant compared to other issues in the world but so significant to Sierra.

The Holy Spirit set off a siren within her each and every time these thoughts came to her. It was as if God was inches away from her ear counter whispering, "**But what did I say about you?**" The warmth of those words, "But what did I say about you?" would always shift her mind to God's word. Lately she'd been stuck on Romans 8:18.

"I consider that our present sufferings are not worth comparing with the glory that will be revealed in us ~ NIV."

The word was a counterweight to the harmful thoughts in her mind. Those self-inflicted seeds that she knew she could never let take root. She didn't know exactly what the scripture in Romans meant but she felt it was telling her that nothing is bad enough to lose your mind over especially when your faith is wrapped around the Master of the Universe and not in the things in this world. And in that moment, she would let the past go and move forward in God's promises.

Knowing how important the word of God was to her she constantly struggled with prioritizing it. Not always feeling like reading a scripture, Sierra considered the task a necessity like the natural ability to exhale. Like inhaling without exhaling, you can't go long without doing one without the other. And she craved the peace that revelations from the Word of God gave her. Like Isaiah 26: 3 declared, "thou will keep him in perfect peace, whose mind is stayed on thee: because he trusteth in thee! ~ KJV."

Chapter 24

The orator was adjusting the focus on the presentation as Sierra entered the Michael Pollack conference room on the south wing of Western Arizona Hospital. That's one thing she loved about the hospital she worked for, WAH. They encouraged all employees to take WAH provided seminars to continue growing their knowledge of health-related issues. The seminars were provided during work hours. The only requirement was for the employee to notify their direct manager, which Sierra did via a calendar reminder where she copied Tom Black as an optional attendant.

"Mental health is one of the most important health topics, and the most overlooked and least discussed between patient and health care provider", the orator with the spikey blond hair boomed as Sierra took a seat on the first empty row she came to in the undersized conference room.

Pivoting toward the right side of the crowded room, he went on to state, "Just like a heart can be diseased, causing heart failure, the pancreas can improperly function resulting in diabetes, or the eye can begin to dim, your emotions, thinking and behavior can shift from healthy to unhealthy".

The spikey-haired orator had the energy of TV personality Dr. Oz and the physique of a 5' 9" yoga instructor. But his command of the content and sense of knowledge on the topic at hand filled the room as if Shaquil Oneal was standing up in a broom closet.

He went on to define mental illness and conditions that fall under the mental illness umbrella. Clicking the presentation controller, he advanced the presentation to the next slide.

"The Mayo Clinic defines mental illness as mental health disorders, including a wide range of mental health conditions — disorders that affect your mood, thinking, and behavior." "Some examples," he went on to explain, "include clinical depression, anxiety disorder, bipolar disorder, dementia, attention-deficit/hyperactivity disorder, schizophrenia, obsessive-compulsive disorder, autism, and post-traumatic stress disorder".

"If we are honest, we all have marginalized many, or at least one of these categories in our lifetime", he said pointing to the presentation with his left hand while scanning the room from left to right with his marble blue eyes.

"How can we normalize, mental health"? Pausing as if he wanted the audience to answer the question. "How is anything normalized"? The room was quiet. He put the pointer down on the podium and slowly walked to the opposite side of the room. No one said a word. Sliding his hands into his navy-blue pants pockets he slowly walked up to the presentation screen. Touching the words on the screen, he said them aloud; "depression, anxiety, bipolar, dementia, ADHD (he paraphrased), schizophrenia, OCD (paraphrasing again), autism, and PTSD".

"Normalizing mental health means we must be willing to discuss mental illness. We must be willing to say these words; as uncomfortable as the words may make you feel, the conditions are real. Not talking about them does not help one heal from the conditions. We must be willing to openly discuss our mental health with someone we trust".

"The CDC defines mental health as," he said while clicking to the next slide, "our emotional, psychological, and social well-being. Mental health affects how we think, feel, and act. It also helps determine how we handle stress, relate to others, and make healthy choices". "Everyone," he said while scanning the room again, "should identify a safe person in their lives to discuss the things that are on their minds. These things are like mazes sometimes", he said pointing to his head," our thoughts get stuck sometime, circulating like a ball stuck in a maze, retracing the same paths repeatedly. No way out, no new path, feeling stuck and out of your control."

The attendants in the seminar seemed to be thinking hard on the orators' words, including Sierra.

"I will conclude with this", he said while clicking to the last slide. The slide was titled, Safe People, Places & Things. "Safe people, places, and things will not violate your trust. Meaning, that what you say to them stops with them. The only time they would violate that trust is to save your life." Eyes wide he said, "if they were told by the person or even hinted that they were going to hurt themselves. Safe PPT's would escalate the situation to others that could help prevent self-harm". He listed examples of PPT as;

- Close Trusted Friends
- Spouses
- Clergy
- Workplace Wellness Resources
- Therapist

Pointing to the table beside the door, "I have compiled a list of clergies, workplace wellness resources, and therapists in the northern Arizona area and online who are all trained in mental health and the treatment of mental illness. I encourage you all to normalize mental health and seek safe PPT if you feel your mental state is not feeling as healthy as you know it should. Thank you all for coming. Please don't forget to sign the attendee list on the way out if you missed it on the way in. We also have a badge reader. If you have your badge, you can scan the card reader on the table beside the attendee list as well. "

Sierra headed toward the table as the room began to empty out. She'd not noticed the attendee list coming in. Thankful that she'd worn her badge, it took all but two seconds for the reader to scan the barcode on the back of her badge. She was also grateful for the information. Never ever thought of speaking with a therapist about her obsessive thoughts concerning the situation she experienced under J.W. Powers. She'd always talked it through with MJ and read God's word in an attempt to dissolve the thoughts if she got stuck in her thoughts and her feelings about it raged out of control. Maybe she thought, grabbing a cardboard flyer from the table with the list of PPT's on it; God was giving her another source to nip this thing in the bud for good. Heading back to her office to wrap up the day she thought on Proverbs 3: 6 (NLT);

"Seek His will in all you do, and He will show you which path to take!"

Chapter 25

Saturday mornings were the absolute best for Sierra. It was the only day of the week when she actually exhaled. She felt for the other six days she was holding on to a tense breath that felt as if she was slowly being released underwater. Drowning with a life jacket on, her old co-worker Mitch would say. Every time he said that she would visibly see someone in the middle of the Atlantic with a life jacket on. Vividly she could imagine the pressure that person must have felt in their chest. As if a hippo was sitting on it refusing to move.

She was intentional about her Saturdays. Intentional about sleeping late, intentional about lingering throughout the day in her pjs. Intentional about what she read, how and what she cleaned around the house, observed on T.V. and even spoke to on the phone. Sundays were reserved for worshiping God, but Saturday was her intentional day to relax. A day to release all the opinions of others that stuck to her like magnets on a fridge. A day to settle her mind from all the overthinking she'd done about everything during the week. A day to put herself first, move at her own pace, or sit and do absolutely nothing.

She regularly used it as an intentional day of gratefulness! God had delivered her from depression and suicide. With much prayer, the guidance of a clinical psychologist, and consistently renewing her mind on the word of God she overcame a heaviness that almost took her out. She was sooooooo grateful to God for keeping her during a time when she was stuck in a fog, void of hope, and lacking vision.

Her posture in life mirrored James 1:2-4; NLT "Dear brothers and sisters, when troubles of any kind come your way, consider it an opportunity for great joy. For you know that when your faith is tested, your endurance has a chance to grow. So let it grow, for when your endurance is fully developed, you will be perfect and complete, needing nothing!"

Knowing she was far from complete and still super needy, needing Jesus like a patient needs an I-V drip in the ICU, she chose to let her endurance grow. Trusting God in the process and grateful and intentional for Saturdays!!

This Saturday she was intentionally catching up on the newest Gospel releases on Spotify while cleaning out the top drawer of her nightstand. Because of her compulsive nature to declutter space, she constantly threw things into that drawer to preserve the neatness of the nightstand top. The accumulated volume of clutter in the drawer had now activated her compulsion.

"Hi, babe," MJ said entering the room with his hat turned backwards. "I see you finally got up."

"Yep, been up for a few hours. You've been in the garage for at least 2 hours yourself. What are you up to today?"

"I promised Max I'd fix the chain on his bike the next weekend I was off. He was up early this morning and so was I," he said with a smile.

Smiling back at him she remembered how handsome she always thought he was in a hat.

"Good! I know Max loved that you remembered without being reminded."

"My boy is just like his mom...."

"And what is that?"

"He doesn't forget NOTHING!!"

They both chuckled as MJ walked out of the room.

"MJ," Sierra called. Seconds later MJ returned to the doorway, eyebrows raised.

"Did you get a chance to speak with Ortega last week?"

"Yeah, heavy stuff. I've been processing and praying, praying and processing since Wednesday.

I was going to mention it to you once God gave me clear direction."

MJ stood in the doorway holding his chin in his hand while massaging his beard.

Silence.

Sierra stared at him, waiting for him to say more.

"And," she finally said after a few more seconds passed.

Physically MJ's 6'4" frame slumped as if the weight of the world was on his shoulders.

Staring back at Sierra, arms now hanging parallel with his body, "It's heavy" he repeated.

"I'm still praying about it'. Spiritually I am aware of what is going on, but Ortega hasn't said exactly what his issue is yet. I trust God will align the timing of them both. I've extended an olive branch. He knows I'm here for him. When Ortega is ready, God will have equipped me with what more I'm to say and do." And with a sigh, he turned and left the room.

Shaking her head in agreement at his comment, she felt a deep love for MJ. Not just because he took great care of them and was so fine, but because he loved and trusted God. His faith got them both through lots of hard times. She knew in church tomorrow he would be listening for a message within the message from Bishop Give, knowing that God speaks through multiple sources. And he would send up some extra prayers not only for his family but for Ortega and his family as well.

MJ's ability to maintain Hope in God continues to be an example for her while managing her own internal struggles.

For that she Thanked God!

Chapter 26

Maria & Ortega (the talk, that took place Sunday night when Ortega arrived home)

Addiction. Maria could barely comprehend what she was hearing. "I'm not stepping out on you Maria. There is no other person. No one is more important to me than you and the girls." Wanting to snicker at the words coming out of Ortega's mouth, at the same time wanting to hear all he had to say, she settled for holding her breath and suppressing all emotions. Especially the urge to roll her eyes considering his actions just didn't line up with what he was saying. Maria slowly exhaled, thinking twice about holding her breath, feeling slightly lightheaded and suddenly out of place. Blinking away her emotions she noticed the air in the kitchen seemed stale, making the room seem unfamiliar and awkward.

While he was struggling to find all his words, the words needed to explain what was on his mind, she was taking him in. Staring at him, she couldn't help but wonder where the man was, she fell in love with all those years ago. His thick black hair had grown past his ears, longer than his normal military buzz cut she was accustomed to seeing him adorn. His orange short-sleeved shirt was saturated in brown sweat stains that looked like samples of elongated amoeba all down the front of his shirt. His carpenter-style blue jeans still showed evidence of his trade, with pens, pads, and a medium-size red measuring tape strapped to each side of his thigh-high pockets. They were soiled in dirt and motor oil and had the faintest smell of dried-up urine. The man before her was a distance difference from who she knew him to be. Normally direct, clean cut, neat, and oozing with confidence.

As if forcing himself to continue, he jerked his head from the prop his hands had provided on the table, looked her in her face, and said, "Crack"! "Crack, Mariaaaaa", his eyes now glistening over, "I'm addicted to crack cocaine"! He spent the next half hour telling her when it happened and how it happened. He told her about his binges, struggles, and how he's been calling out to God for help, to deliver him from this addiction and all the shame and self-disappointment linked to it. That he didn't know how to overcome it, but he was sure he didn't want to continue down the road he was on. Or continue avoiding her and the girls, even in his shame.

Continuing to take shallow breaths in the stale kitchen, as he told her months of details, she didn't have the strength to do anything more than stand planted on the opposite side of the island, as still and stoic as an oak tree.

Addiction. Ortega was blown away with himself, that he finally had the courage to look his situation dead in the eyeballs and give it a name. Addiction. He couldn't read Maria's reaction to what he was saying but he knew she heard him because she was as motionless as a statute. He could never remember a time when Maria was at a standstill while awoke. His wife, the mother of his four children, was always on the move. Cooking, cleaning, rearing their girls. Chauffeuring them around town, making sure he had everything he needed, and making their house a home. If they were in the kitchen as a family, she'd normally be drinking coffee and checking homework, rolling out cornmeal for tortillas and running dishwater, or sweeping the floor and instructing the girls how to bake tres leche cupcakes. Even in that moment he thought of Maria with love and compassion in his heart and imagined if there were pictures in the bible for some of the verses, he was familiar with Maria's picture would surely be pinned to Proverbs 31: 27 ~ (NIV)

"She watches over the affairs of her household and does not eat the bread of idleness".

He held deep admiration for her. Thinking how lucky a man he was to be married to a friend and lover as beautiful and as youthful looking as his Maria. Dropping his head in his hand he fought to contain his emotions. He wanted to cry. He felt a swelling in his chest like the swells of the Red Sea awaiting the passing of the children of Israel escaping Pharos army. A deep, earthy cry as from the sorrows of losing your closest sibling. Tears so sorrowful they make your jaws ache; your eyes burn and voice hoarse from the force of the converted pain. Steading himself in the palm of his own hands, he gathered up his emotions and settled himself as if he were a volcano refusing to erupt. And for the next thirty minutes, he downloaded all he'd experienced in the past months in his crack cocaine addiction.

When Ortega finished, Maria finally moved. She moved toward Ortega and embraced him with all the love she had. In her kitchen that had become stale and felt so unfamiliar, Ortega's embrace was familiar. The hard shell that began to encompass her heart over the months had begun to soften. She didn't know how she would help him, but she knew for sure she loved him and intended to do all she could to help him defeat his addiction.

In the embrace, Maria was flooded with so many emotions and questions. Ortega, feeling the love through the embrace still felt a boatload of fear and shame. Literally holding on to each other for life, they held the embrace for what seemed like hours. Neither knowing what to say or the next steps to take from this point.

There were many tears. Following their long embrace Sunday night when Ortega finally came home, they worked in silence cleaning up the kitchen. The only ten words spoken by Maria were, "We will tell the girls your home in the morning". Ortega simply bowed his head, yes, in agreement. Placing the final dish in the dishwasher, she turned off the kitchen light and instructed him to head to their room while she tucked the girls in bed.

Ten minutes later she was back in the room. Ortega had taken his clothes off and heading for the shower in their on-suit.

Maria sat on the edge of the bed waiting for his shower to end. She had unanswered questions she didn't feel she could sleep on.

The warm water was soothing, Ortega enjoyed it and used it as an excuse to avoid Maria as long as possible. He knew his wife and knew she was not sleep. As he was washing the shampoo from his hair questions started racing through his head. What more did she want to know, he thought. Was she afraid of him? Surely, she didn't trust him... his mind wandered on. Did she really want the girls to know he was home? How much of this should they be made aware of? Could he do this, be free of this addiction, and choose his family again as the priority and not himself? Was Maria really woke waiting on him or in there hiding all the valuables? Shame evaded his mind again. Drying off, he pulled on his undies and opened the bathroom door to face the inevitable.

Finally, she thought, as she anxiously shifted her weight. Unconsciously Maria had been leaning forward toward the bathroom door with her hands propped on her knees. Unsure why the door opening startled her, she quickly pulled herself upright and maneuvered until her back was leaning against the headboard. As he walked to get into bed, she unloaded her questions.

"Are there others from your crew addicted?" He took a deep breath as if to begin to answer but she continued. "How could you be so trusting, sharing anything, much less drugs, with a stranger like that? Where was MJ when all of this was going down? How could he not have seen that something was going on with you, that something was not right? It's been months. Is this all? Are there other drugs, something other than cocaine?"

Now in the bed under the covers, Ortega dropped his eyes to stare at his hands, the only thing besides his head, lying outside of the cover. He was prostrate in bed, feeling like a thirteen-thousand-pound elephant was hovering over his chest intending to sit. Never lifting his head, he opened his mouth, attempting to answer yet she continued.

"Have you ever had this mess in my home, around our kids?" Eyes now bugged, Maria was doing all she could to wrangle her emotions and keep her voice low so as not to startle the girls. "Have you?" she hissed. He shook his head no, therefore she continued. "What are you going to do? How are you going to get delivered from this mess? What are WE going to do? Oh my god, I need a job. We could lose our home? How are we going to provide for the girls? When was the last time you used it? Are you feeling like you need some NOW!"

Maria was now quiet, back against the headboard, one leg hanging off the side of the bed, staring intently at Ortega with glossy eyes. Glossy eyes that soon gave way to silent tears, never looking away from him. "Ricco," she said very softly, almost at a whisper. "Ricco Ortega, "how are we going to get through this"? He reached out and touched her knee, the one pointing toward him. She only called him Ricco when she was seriously hurt. Blinking back his own tears he opened his mouth to find the words, and answer, anything. Nothing, silence. His throat burned, fighting to maintain his emotions dried out his mouth and the emotions stored themselves there. He tried swallowing, but it felt like he was attempting to swallow a handful of cotton balls, he was unsuccessful.

Unsuccessful at swallowing, unsuccessful at answering any question that required him to make a sound, form a word, or require him to speak. All he could do was pat her leg. Pat her leg and allow his emotions to run out his eyes, down his face, past his ears, and puddle on the cover. With her clothes still on Maria moved from the edge of the bed to under the cover. Ortega opened his arms, and she laid her head in the pit of his arm continuing to cry. They both lie with heavy hearts and monsoon tears holding each other. They could neither find words for a prayer nor remember a scripture to soothe their minds as they lay in bed weeping and mentally tussling with the situation at hand.

When Jesus speaks in John 14:26 (NLT), He said, "But when the Father sends the Advocate as my representative –that is the Holy Spirit – he will teach you everything and will remind you of everything I have told you."

So as they lay, weeping, at a loss for words or deeds on how to seek peace, the Holy Spirit camped around them, filling their bedroom and reminding them both of what God said in his word.

Psalm 56: 3 (NIV) ~ "When I am afraid, I put my trust in you."

Psalm 56: 8 (NLT) ~ "God keep track of all my sorrows, He collected all my tears in His bottle. He recorded each one in His book. 9 (NLT) ~ My enemies will retreat when I call to You for help. This I know, God is on my side!"

The spirit kept whispering these verses to them both until they drifted off to sleep. As if God had enclosed them in a cocoon during the night, they neither moved, tossed, or woke until the next morning. Completely rested and with a renewed sense of hope.

Maria woke, prayed, showered, and headed out to the kitchen to prepare breakfast for her family. It was the first day of the school week. Life doesn't stop because hard issues trespass into it, this Maria knew. Ortega dressed for work and went to wake the girls. Happy squills of "Daddy your home" could be heard across their home as Maria prepared oatmeal and scrambled eggs for breakfast. Placing breakfast on the table, she turned and proceeded to fix bagged lunches. Everyone was getting peanut butter and grape jelly sandwiches today, with sliced apples and Sponge Bob peach yogurt. Mini Dasni water bottles would have to do for today. Turning to the fridge she wrote, boxed orange Hi C on the grocery list stuck to the door.

As her family wrapped up breakfast and the girls chatted with their dad, Maria sat and silently prayed. "Thank you, God, for loving us in spite of ourselves. I do not know what to do next, but I know you do. I don't know what to say, do, ask, or not ask but I know you do. Keep holding me in the palm of your hand, please God, keep directing my heart, and please don't let my ear stop hearing your direction. I plead the blood of Jesus over my family. Over my girls as they live this thing out with us. Please raise up a standard on their behalf to shield them from all hurt, harm, incident, or danger. We know you don't override our will, but please give Ortega the strength to overcome this addiction. And Lord please send people our way that can help us win the battle and claim this victory. In Jesus name, I pray. Amen"!

"Time to go, little ladies," she said. They all hugged their dad, grabbed their book bags, and headed out the door.

"I'll be right there," Maria said to Alondra, who was the last one out the door.

"What do you plan to do today," she said turning to Ortega.

"Go to work. MJ sensed something was off. Wednesday, he told me he was a safe place; whatever I was going through he would be there for me. I'm going to take him up on that".

So, all day, Maria wrestled with her thoughts and emotions. Even passing by Ortega's worksite a few times to check if his car was there. Everywhere she went, it was on her mind. At the grocery store she almost forgot to pick up the girl's drinks for lunch the rest of the week because she was so distracted with her thoughts. Back home, she prepared dinner, cleaned the house, and went through Ortega's dirty clothes from the night before. Paranoid the entire time thinking she would find traces of drugs in or on his clothes. The whole situation had her thoughts hostage.

I need a good sweat she thought. School dismisses at 2:45 pm. Looking at the clock it was just 1:15 pm. Quickly remembering she didn't have to pick the girls up until 4 pm today since Mondays they have Code Ninjas after school.

After the revelation last night, Maria needed every available hour today to work through her thoughts and emotions.

Turning off the stove, she headed for her room and changed into her workout clothes. Heading to the YMCA, she hoped she could find a good step class and then she would race for 30 minutes on the elliptical. Snapping her fingers, headphones, she thought. Looking around the vehicle they were nowhere to be found. Glove box she thought.

After parking near the Y entrance, she checked the glove box. Bingo! Thank God for small miracles she thought. Grabbing the hot pink birthday gift from the girls, she placed them around her neck, locked the doors, and entered the gym. Time to tap in!

By the time she had jumped, danced, stepped, and raced on the elliptical machine, blasting her Christian music the entire time, she felt free of the backpack of emotions she started the day with. Completely free, maybe not but definitely not consumed with the weight of anxiety and fear.

She was only left with the knowledge of the situation and anticipation and hope of God's answer to it.

And in that mindset, she headed to pick the girls up from their after-school program.

Picking the girls up from school, she was thankful for the Monday after-school activity they begged to participate in. Code Ninjas of Scottsdale partnered with the school system to offer the program to all Pre-K through 8th graders. God bless whoever it is that has the patience to teach these little ones how to write computer code, Maria had said when she was signing them up. Only certain schools acted as host locations depending on the size of their computer labs. Thankfully Wimble Elementary was a good size school with a very large computer lab. Great size to host Code Ninjas for up to seventy-five students. Unlike some parents, there was no need for Maria to worry about transport after school, the Ortega girls could just walk from homeroom to the lab. It was only one day per week and well worth it, really all they could afford at $20 per child to attend, this extra hour of activity after school was a small monthly expense for the Ortega family. The girls were learning a lot about STEM – science technology, engineering, and mathematics. Maria knew they were gaining critical thinking and problem-solving skills that could be used in any area of their lives. They, on the other hand were simply excited about the cool things they learned on the computer each week and were very excited about building the robot, the final project coming up in a few weeks.

But today the program was a life saver.

Chapter 27

The start of the work week was sometimes rough, but today MJ rose early and was at the job site before the sun was up. Even beating Nishnea's food truck which was always the first person at the site on Mondays. Prepping to serve her homemade hot buttermilk biscuits. They were a hit at the work site. She offered sausage biscuits or bacon biscuits with a cup of coffee for $3. She believed a hearty breakfast made for the start of a great work week.

About an hour ahead of his normal daily schedule he decided to walk and pray. So anxious about what he felt God was going to do today he'd not considered that leaving the house as early as he had would have him outside in the dark. Spring was just approaching. In another three weeks, it would be light by this time, but today it was not. Getting out of the truck, thinking he'd wasted more time than necessary thinking about how dark it was, he took a deep breath of the crisp air that singled the beginning of spring. Determined to be aligned with words God would have him to say today he took off walking around the perimeter of the parking lot for the next thirty minutes praying the entire time in his holy language.

Leaving the house after Maria and the girls this morning Ortega felt grateful but also heavy. As he drove into work a heaviness in his heart seemed to rise up through the base of his chin, spread out to his shoulders and down his arms to his wrist like fear. All he could think about was her last question, what do you plan to do today? Rightfully she doesn't trust me, but worst of all he thought, I've now shifted my burden to her. Lord I've faltered big time and...

The Holy Spirit interrupted his thoughts as he got closer to the work site:

Remember how I protected Elijah from the heaviness of his circumstance. 1 King 19:5-9 (NIV)

"5 Then he lay down under the bush and fell asleep. All at once an angel touched him and said, "Get up and eat." 6 He looked around, and there by his head was some bread baked over hot coals, and a jar of water. He ate and drank and then lay down again. 7 The angel of the Lord came back a second time and touched him and said, "Get up and eat, for the journey is too much for you." 8 So he got up and ate and drank. Strengthened by that food, he traveled forty days and forty nights until he reached Horeb, the mountain of God. 9 There he went into a cave and spent the night."

The Holy Spirit continued, "Know that even though you faltered, God will strengthen you and Maria for the journey ahead. The journey will not be easy but know I am with you, ready to walk with you through it all."

As he parked, he still felt the heaviness and fear but was also reassured that God had not forsaken him even though he continued to turn his back on God. That thought alone was sobering and gave him a glimmer of hope packed in with fear and heaviness. Sitting in the car, the engine off but keys still in the ignition, he was also overcome with thoughts of how he would physically make it through the day. He was already starting to feel the effects of the absence of the drug in his system. His emotions were out of balance, and he now had a physical urge starting to emerge resembling a cramp in one's calf, now just a little muscle tightness but at any unidentified moment could turn to pain.

Just as he was about to debate whether he would stay or go, he spotted MJ walking through the parking lot down the row of spaces he was parked in.

MJ walked right up to his parked car, stopping at the driver-side front bumper. With his hands resting in the pockets of his warm clay colored Carhart vest, he gave Ortega the warmest smile and mouthed good morning.

Straying far from God does not mean we do not know His word; more often than not, it means that we failed to obey it. The word was definitely with Ortega.

Staring back at MJ, Ortega thought of a scripture from one of his favorite books in the bible; Proverbs. Proverbs 17:17 (NLT) stated, "A friend is always loyal, and a brother is born to help in time of need."

He was not sure what MJ intended to tell him this morning, but looking at him waiting on him to get out of the car he felt a brotherly love oozing from this man who was his boss partner that had become his friend. And he could really use a friend, a friend that's like a brother right now in his life.

"Good to see you this morning man," MJ beamed as Ortega reluctantly exited his car. Giving each other the one-arm man hug greeting MJ got right to the point.

"You've been on my heart since our last conversation. I hope you know I am sincere when I say I am a safe space O man. I love you like a brother and want to see you succeed in all you do. I prayed about this thing, and God gave me some direction that will help you walk this thing out and come out on the other end, an overcomer. Do I think it will be a cakewalk? No, not at all. Will I be here with you and your family every step of the way, yes, if you allow me."

Ortega lowered his head, leaned against the hood of his car, then sat and slid back onto it. "I told...," he started, his words then trailed off. "I told Maria about my issue last night." "This thing has me so, so...," he turned his head, looking away from MJ off into the distant empty part of the parking lot, "so upside-down." "I'm losing myself, man, and truly don't know what to do. I am addicted to crack cocaine. I know I don't want to be like this." Looking down at his chest, "I don't want to feel like this, physically urging for something I mentally know I should not. Feeling emotionally bankrupt from this internal and external war, I'm trying to fight, and at every turn knowing I am losing the battle. God warned me and I ignored the alarm. Now I'm a drug addict, a disobedient Christian, needing God to make this path I made crooked, straight again. Maria is distraught and worried; my little girls are confused yet I feel

God still loves me even though I can't see why! Knowing that," he looked directly at MJ," Is that offer to help still on the table?"

Facing Ortega, MJ patted his shoulder and sat beside him on the hood. "Remember Romans 2:11 (NIV) "'For God does not show favoritism.'" He loves us all the same. We can't do anything to make Him love us or not love us. We are all redeemed because of his grace."

Holding his knee as he sat on the hood of the car MJ turned to Ortega and said, "God will guide you on this journey back to self. Fight like David in the bible did in every battle he fought to win. After much prayer", MJ continued as he now propped his elbows on his knees, "God has a way of giving us revelations. He gave me a revelation this weekend of what you are dealing with and nudged my memory reminding me that our health insurance has a rider in it that supports addiction treatment. It covers the full cost of live-in treatment facilities; 30 days (about four and a half weeks) for facilities outside of our network and 60 days (about two months) for facilities within our network."

"Over the weekend I researched facilities that are in our network. I was surprised at how many there were, yet I found one in Las Vegas, Nevada, that's top-rated and reported to be highly effective."

Hearing MJ's words, Ortega sensed a glimmer of light in the midst of this nightmare. For the first time all morning, the heaviness he felt seemed to faintly evaporate. Help, he thought. Someone could help me. He looked at MJ, and as MJ read his next thought he continued with equally good news.

"Man don't worry about your family, MJ continued. I know Maria is a stay-at-home mom and that you are the single source of income for your family. If you accept this help, I will commit to continuing your pay, which will be equal to your normal 40 hours per week for up to 60 days. Your finances will not be impacted, and you can begin to get the help you need to overcome this addiction."

Turning away from MJ, Ortega's tears freely streamed down his face. He felt surrounded, a fullness encompassing him as if he was bobbing around in a backyard swimming pool, the presence of God. They sat in silence marinating in all MJ just said for the next few minutes.

"Thank you." Thank you was all Ortega could say. Through his tears, he kept saying thank you! "We will get through this; we will get through this together man!"

Ortega gladly accepted MJ's offer. There were some administrative things that had to be put in place. Checking with Ortega, MJ asked if he could physically make it through the workday. He needed to make a call to the third-party company that handled his human resources paperwork for compensation and pay to get the ball rolling on all he discussed with Ortega earlier. The goal would be to have all plans locked and loaded by the end of their workday at 3:30 pm. "Yes," he said, "I will be okay," Ortega told himself he would fight this aching in his body like the angels fight for us daily to get to the door of his healing. "3:30 he said aloud, yes, I can make it."

Chapter 28

Ortega spent 60 days in an addiction treatment center in Las Vegas Nevada. He walked through the door that aided in his healing the very next day after the encounter with MJ.

Maria was so overcome with joy after hearing the news after Ortega returned from work that night that she could not help but praise God. Running into her bedroom bathroom she let out a Hallelujah from the depths of her soul. Over and over again, she yelled, "Hallelujah, hallelujah, hallelujah!" Then she started praising His name; "Wonderful Counselor, Might God, Everlasting Father, Prince of Peace, the Great I AM, Bread of Life, Living Water, All Mighty God, the King of Kings, Unmatched Father, Our God You are Great and greatly to be praised!"

The peace she felt in this moment didn't align with any other peace she had ever felt. In the midst of her peace about the situation there were still waves of uncertainty attempting to poke holes in her optimistic posture. But she chose to believe God would work a miracle despite how she felt!

She helped Ortega pack his things that very night. They felt for true healing to take place they had to start being transparent now and pledged to be as truthful as possible with the girls from this point forward.

That night, they shared with the girls as much as was age appropriate 'daddy's struggle'. Alondra-12, Liliana-10, Carmen-7 and Isabella-4 walked away from the conversation

125

with an understanding that Daddy was struggling to focus on the things that were important to him and needed to be away for a while why he worked with people who would help him get his focus back.

They cried but understood since this seemed to be very important to their father, considering he cried the entire time he explained it to them. Tuesday morning, they all hugged and kissed him goodbye. Maria dropped them off at school and she and Ortega took the 3-hour drive to the facility in Las Vegas.

They arranged for Sierra to pick the girls up after school and MJ would meet them at the facility in Vegas at 10 am.

God orchestrated the perfect melody that day. Ortega was overcome with emotions as he learned from the administration team at the facility that the certified clinicians were trained at some of the top schools and have worked with people from every walk of life, from the everyday Joe to A-list celebrities. Sierra was humbled to see the grounds and campus reflect the quality and upkeep of a five-star hotel and was ever-so-grateful to have the support of MJ. Like family he was there to help fill in the gaps; what she didn't understand, he did. What she could not answer, he did. Content she could not digest, he did.

Between all that God was stirring up and the help and assistance of MJ and Sierra, Maria felt hopeful.

She knew Ortega would continue to need a healthy support system when he returned home, and she was willing to do the work to ensure she understood what support for drug addicts looked like. Determined to start now, she would not be figuring it out when Ortega returned home. He was worth the effort; her family was worth it as well, and she was committed to doing all she could to ensure they all succeeded!

During those 60 days, Ortega received the addiction treatment he needed. All the while, his pay continued to be directly deposited so Maria could continue to take care of home expenses, and the addiction treatment fees were 100% covered by their insurance just as MJ said they would be.

Maria and the girls visited Ortega every two weeks. Neither Ortega nor Maria thought it appropriate for the girls to visit him on the facilities campus. Ortega would take a facility shuttle to the LVN mall and meet Maria and the girls there. There was plenty of space to walk around, a play area for the kids to play and many options in the food court, and a few restaurants all on site. They enjoyed each other for hours before heading back to the facility and home.

MJ and Sierra checked on Maria and the girls from time to time, and before long the 60 days had passed, and Ortega was home.

Ortega had now been without the drug for 60 days. He learned at the facility that he needed to take one day at a time, to build a disciplined routine for his day, and to continue, to meet with his recovery counselor weekly. And most importantly continue to maintain abstinence from the drug.

He was able to come back home and get right back to work. MJ treated him as if he never left. The responsibilities he had as Managing Electrician continued. When he was away, MJ reached out to Bishop Give and learned that there was a group for former addicts at the church called Gods Road to Recovery that meet every two weeks. Ortega was eager to connect with the group, glad God had provided him with yet another resource to help keep the right focus.

He was optimistic about his recovery but had learned enough from his stay in Las Vegas to know not to be naive about his recovery. He knew he would be tempted but was determined to overcome temptation through God's word, group discussions, and continued therapy with his addiction clinician. Another blessing God bestowed on him; the clinician was also covered under his insurance for the next 12 months!! Look at God, he thought.

Ortega also pledged to himself to be conscious of God's nudging. Now realizing that's the Holy Spirit, his internal siren. He is always on watch, ready to alert him on things that are and that are not God's perfect will for his life. Also, to continue to trust in his favorite verse, Jeremiah 32:27 (KJV) "Behold, I am the Lord, the God of all flesh. Is there anything too hard for me?" "Absolutely not," Ortega said aloud. "Absolutely nothing is too hard for God!"

Sirens

Chapter 29

"MJ, thank you for loving us all, Hun. Me, Max, Ortega and his family, your crew, members at church, and those in the community. If you don't mind, I'm going to do a little loving on myself as well and do more to support my mental health! Seeing what Maria and Ortega are going through I just don't want to miss anything God is nudging me to do anymore."

"Like a siren, for years, he's been telling me I didn't die on the cross for others He did. To lay these burdens down. I think talking them out with a neutral person will be helpful. I know you and a clinician helped me before when I overcame the initial depression from the J. W. Power incident. I should talk to someone again. More regularly this time, a professional."

"I'm going to look up a family therapist and schedule a session."

"Sierra, that is excellent news. I want you to feel free to do whatever you think you need to for your complete health.

So, you can always clearly hear the sirens of life."

The End!

About the Author

Sadie Goodloe resides in Garner, NC and is an avid reader and worshiper. She was educated in and currently works in technology. *Sirens* is her first published book. She has two adult sons Justice and Mysta and has been married to her college sweetheart, Alle, for over twenty years. She enjoys caring for her family, including her mom Joann, through acts of service. She also enjoys serving in the church where needed and desires to complete and publish other works of Christian fiction. Keep an eye out for future book releases.

Scripture Reference

1 Corinthians	6:19
1 Corinthians	13:4-8
1 Corinthians	13:5-7
1 King	19:5-9
2 Corinthians	5:8
Deuteronomy	6:4-6
Galatians	6:1-2
Hebrew	10:38
Isaiah	61:3
Isaiah	26:3
James	1:2-4
Jeremiah	32:27
John	14:26
Mark	4:39
Proverbs	10:22
Proverbs	3:6
Proverbs	31:27
Proverbs	17:17
Psalm	30:2
Psalm	56:3
Psalm	56:8
Romans	8:18
Romans	2:11

Made in the USA
Columbia, SC
06 October 2024

43125190R00076